ROAD TO ELYSIUM

By
Kay A. Oliver

"Words can't express how much I enjoyed this book. This is the final book and it makes me sad that it is ending but what a doozy of a finale. Kay Oliver excellent as always! ~E. Sanders

"The author did a great job. I would thoroughly recommend this book to all as it has a bit of everything worked in with a clearly well-researched and clever plot. Highly recommend to anyone and Really wonderful. Thank you Kay Oliver." ~ A. Bolte

Other fine books by
Kay A. Oliver

Disturbed Tombs: Dr. Kaili Worthy Series Book 1
A Historical Fiction – Mystery
Previously published as Voice of A Mummy: Dr. Kaili Worthy Series

Grave Disturbances: Dr. Kaili Worthy Series Book 2
A Historical Fiction - Mystery

Shooter's Treasure
Mystery, Contemporary Romance

Sisters In Cold Blood: An Unwanted Sisterhood
Mystery, Thriller, Suspense

Go to KayAOliver.com for more
from this award-winning author

QUOTES

"The key to change ... is to let go of fear."

– Rosanne Cash

"If you don't like something, change it. If you can't change it, change your attitude."

– Maya Angelou

"Change is the law of life and those who look only to the past or present are certain to miss the future."

– John F. Kennedy

DEDICATION

This book is dedicated to all those individuals who give of themselves in a powerful quiet pursuit of spreading love and kindness among others. These are the people we all know who help others without seeking rewards or notoriety for their actions. They are altruistic individuals. They do what is right without question. These special people would do everything anonymously if given the option. Someone of this caliber may have helped you at one time, and you never knew it. They don't require praise and certainly do not want to be the center of attention for their selfless deeds.

***

"Do everything you do with the intent of love. Even breathing is an act of love for your own body. Help others to breath." Kay A. Oliver

PREFACE

BALANCING DAVID

by Kay Oliver © 2009

The statue of David is known throughout the world as one of the greatest masterpieces of all time and probably the most famous statue ever. Michelangelo was commissioned in 1501 to create this wondrous work for decoration of the Cathedral in Florence. Arte della Lana, a wool merchant, is the person who commissioned the artist.

Michelangelo was given a solid block of marble in which an artist before him, Agostino di Duccio, had already attempted a goliath statue of his own forty years earlier but never completed the project.

Michelangelo began to chisel away. Piece by piece of the unwanted marble fell away as more of the David that Michelangelo envisioned emerged from the stone.

Unlike the David's before him, this David was not the conquering hero or the self-assured warrior that most portray him as, but rather the young David who stood before a crowd of people that were jeering him as a giant was mocking him.

Most of us can understand what that David would be feeling at that moment in time. Everyone has experiences of being up against a goliath, or not being worthy of the fight. We all question if we can even succeed at our own quests in life. We all know that our bodies and minds are not the perfection that Michelangelo's David represents.

Although one could argue that it is most likely David's body and frame of mind was never flawless either. After all, the statue stands for strength and determination. The pose of David, along with his muscular physique, demonstrates power and creates a balance of truth, meaning, and emotion. Afterall, it is a piece of art.

Then I have to ask, what more of a marvel is there than a human being, whose body can change, who can learn, and thrive, and lives, unlike Michelangelo's great David?

Even with all our human flaws, we have the ability to change, to transform, to improve every day we are alive. There is so much good in us, and so many parts of us worth loving. We need to know we are not marble.

Often, we forget that Michelangelo never chiseled away a part of the marble he wanted to save. Instead, he teaches us that we need to learn what to get rid of and what to hold on to. As we live, we need to value ourselves greater. We need the courage to seek out new adventures, and new wisdom.

We are not our circumstances, but rather how we answer to them. What is essential is *who* we are, how we live our lives, and that we keep in balance.

David was a masterpiece that took Michelangelo years to complete. One could say his David was a work of love. The statue of David will never compare to you or I. Unlike the frozen marble David, we travel through time changing, loving, learning, experiencing, and best of all – being who we are. Unlike David, we can alter ourselves, expand, and move forward.

We are more perfect than David. More beautiful than David. But like the marble he was sculpted from, we can be just as stubborn in accepting who we tell ourselves we are. We can be just as frozen in who we are as David has been since 1501.

Transformation can be scary because we

do not know the outcome of taking those steps. Keeping our minds and hearts open, someone could come into your life and change it for the better. We need to receive and give love. We need to be more than a statue at any given time.

ROAD TO ELYSIUM

By Kay A. Oliver

CHAPTER ONE

Sitting in his sanctuary - his living room - Ken wonders why he is still living when ending it all sounds like the better option. Life has not shown mercy on him. The scars on his body he would never trade away, but the scar in his heart is killing him and not fast enough.

Ken takes refuge in his Chicago home by spending evenings in front of the TV, stretching out on his old chestnut brown leather lounge chair. It is where he spends most of his time in the house when he is not at work. There are nights he naps there if he sleeps at all. Most nights, he spends in the restless wonder of what he could have done differently to protect his family. His sleeplessness over the last couple of years is the price he pays for his sorrow.

Two nights earlier, the living room lamp bulb blew. Being too lazy to fix it, Ken started sitting in the dark once nightfall hits. The only ambient glow comes from the streetlight in front of the house next door. This particular night he is sitting in front of the TV with the volume on low. He is pressed into his brown leather lounger, transfixed into space as he runs memories of his wife and child through his mind. The memories are pleasant.

Grief is his daily companion. A purgatory he holds onto as he shuffles through his family photos. Holding onto an old photo of his wife and son, he memorizes every detail of their faces for fear of forgetting. He prefers to review photos, as the images are like statues, allowing Ken to take in every detail.

Much has not changed from that day. He has not taken the time to go through anything in the house. It is as if time has frozen between the walls while the world goes on without him. His child's room remains untouched after all this time. Many of his wife's personal effects are still all around the house. The only thing that keeps Ken alive is the fear his death would take these memories with him, and there would be nothing left of her or any proof that his baby ever lived.

This particular evening, Ken's mood is more melancholy than usual. The TV nightly news is going through the normal ritual of listing all the impending disasters, killer bug reports and other uplifting information. Ken is not paying attention to any of the reports since he only keeps the television on for background noise, so the house is not so silent.

Crash!

Ken immediately leaps from his chair, grabs his handgun from the side table and heads toward his kitchen back door leaving his lights off. He could easily see within his house as his eyes were already attuned to using only the street light beams coming in from the side windows to guide him. Turning on a light would only warn his intruders.

He knows he will try to keep the intruders

out as he listens to the repeating kicks against the wooden door to break through. He stands still and quiets to mimic the fact the intruders must be thinking that no one is home.

A huge clatter came next as he witnessed his kitchen door crashing open. It only takes a few seconds before the door is open wide so that two dark silhouetted figures can enter his house.

"Stop right there." He yells.

The taller of the two figures swings around and fire a shot off, missing Ken completely. Ken fires back, hitting the intruder in the right side of his chest. Then the taller silhouette hits the ground as a second smaller one takes cover crouching next to the bottom kitchen cabinets and extending his hand in a futile attempt to stop any bullets coming his way.

"Don't move, or I will shoot you," Ken orders the second intruder. Ken believes he has secured the intrusion into his home and flips on the kitchen lights. No one else seems to be with these two young men. Ken phones 9-1-1 and reports the event.

"Hello. Police"

"Yes, how can we help you?" the dispatcher asks

"Two people have broken into my house. One has been shot, and the other is sitting on my kitchen floor."

"Do you need paramedics?"

"Yes. Please send an ambulance too." Ken informs the dispatcher of the home address and cross the streets.

Keeping his eyes on both intruders, Ken continues to answer all of the dispatcher's questions.

"How did someone get shot?"

"He shot at me first, and I returned fire. It appears that I hit him in the upper chest area. Please hurry."

Keeping the gun pointed at the crouched

intruder, who is now down on the ground, Ken leans forward slightly to study the trespassers. To Ken's amazement, both intruders were just children. Teenagers, to be exact.

Ken can now hear the sirens. He knows the officers will be there shortly. Knowing that doesn't stop his concern for the young man he shot. Ken is a little mad at himself for having taken an action that caused him to shoot a teenager, even though the intruder shot at him first. "Hang on. They are almost here."

Knowing that the police would arrive first, he is fully aware of the need to watch himself and ensure he is not mistaken as one of the intruders. Several walls now reflect the red and blue police car lights. Ken can hear the officers out in the yard.

Yelling out to the officers, Ken says, "In here. They are both in here, and one is injured."

Ken knows to place his gun on the table and moves away a little. Raising both arms, he made no sudden moves so the police would know he meant no harm.

As the police came in, one could be heard talking on his radio. "We have two suspects; one has been shot and needs an ambulance immediately."

The second officer is handcuffing the young man huddling on the kitchen floor while the other officer attempts to put pressure on the gunshot wound of the other suspect. After a minute, the gunshot wound to his chest becomes fatal.

"What is your name?" the officer asks the surviving intruder.

"Cody Hill."

"Your friend?" The officer askes as he nods nodded his head toward the shot suspect lying motionless on the kitchen floor.

"That is James Burns."

"And what were you two up to?"

"We thought no one was home," Cody professes.

"That doesn't answer my question." The

officer states with frustration.

"Robbing the house."

The officer stops questioning the young man and comes to Ken to get his story and personal information. "Hi. I am Ken Hines. I live here. I was at home when I heard noises at my back door. The taller one entered first. I told him to freeze, but he spun around and shot at me."

The officer is feverishly taking notes. Then he looks down where the young man still lay and then turns to look at the opposing wall behind Ken. There it was. The bullet hole.

"He missed you. You don't look injured."

"Um, yes, he did." Ken answers. Hoping that wasn't an issue.

Looking over at the officer still applying CPR next to the shot intruder, the officer looks back at Ken and then at the wall behind him, lining up where the bullet could have gone. "Is that a bullet hole over there?"

Turning around, Ken sees the new hole in his wall. "Yes," Ken confirms.

"We will make sure forensics tags it." Turning his attention back to Ken, the officer continues. "We will need to take your gun as well."

"Yes, sir. I understand." Ken knows he has another gun. Knowing the police will only hold it for a few days, he is of little concern.

Once police signal it is clear, the EMTs enter the room and begin administering medical protocol to the injured intruder. They move quickly. Before Ken knows it, the young man is rushed to the ambulance.

"Mr. Hines, if you could step outside to let forensics do their job." The officer asks as he escorts Ken out the back door. Running into one of the forensic team members, the officer directs them to the opposing wall where the bullet hole was and askes for pictures and the recovery of the bullet. "Make sure that happens, thanks," the officer commands.

Ken walks over and sits in his lawn chair. The nighttime air feels a little brisk against his sweaty skin. Ken did not realize he was sweating. It must have been nerves. He has never had to fire on a teenager before. That is not something he had ever had to do when he was in the military. He had heard stories of the opposing side having very young soldiers during war and how others in his unit found that shooting a young person messes with your mind. Now he was experiencing a little bit of that, minus the war.

Sitting there for the next few hours, he watches as different people go in and out of his house. The forensic team took pictures of everything as they step over the blood on the kitchen floor. His quiet evening has turned into anything but. For Ken, it did not matter how long it took the forensic team to finish since he never really sleeps.

A female officer soon approaches him. "We are almost done. Thank you for your patience. The other officer said he had already got all your information. We will call you or come by if we need anything further."

"Thanks. Once you leave, can I clean up?"

"We have all the images and samples we need. We retrieved the bullet from the wall as well. You can do whatever you need to do."

"Appreciate it."

As the last forensic team members, all dressed in their light blue jumpers, blue slipper covers, and white hairnets, finally walks out the door, Ken just sits there as they walk down his driveway. He waits a minute before going back to his house. He knows the blood would still be there and does not want to deal with it right now. Rising slowly, he heads back into his traumatized sanctuary.

He grabs the first kitchen towel he sees and tosses it over the blood. Ken heads to the linen closet on the other side of the kitchen, grabbing more old towels and tossing them to the floor. He decides to deal with everything in the morning and heads back to his living room chair. He would have to fix the back door as well. He would search his phone for repair companies and leave a message for the emergency service. It would be another night of no sleep.

CHAPTER TWO

Calling into work, Ken lets his associate partner know he will be late.

"Hello, Morgan. Sorry, I will be in later today. A couple of kids tried to break into my house last night through my kitchen door. I need to wait for the repair guy to show up. Can you hold the fort down?"

"Sure thing, boss," Morgan replies.

After hanging up the phone, he turns the TV volume up as the local morning news talks about how the police captured the persons responsible for recent break-ins throughout the county.

Catching his full attention, Ken sees the image of the young man who had been at his house just hours before. His face fills the screen as the news continues to report that his cohort has died from the injuries attained during the attempted robbery. The fear in the young man's eyes fills Ken's heart. Bold red letters are showing the young man's name scroll by on the bottom of the monitor.

Ken starts to wonder how someone would end up breaking into homes at a young age. The young man did not live that far away from his house. Though it wasn't the same neighborhood, it was close enough for Ken to consider it the same. The young man would be his son's age if he were still alive today. The difference between the two was not lost on Ken. Ken becomes instantly attached to the young man on the screen. He feels drawn to his circumstances and wonders if he can help somehow.

Right then, a truck pulls up outside his house. Ken is happy that the repair guy showed up on time. Ken smiles a little as he notices that the repair person looks strong and is built like a lumberjack. Popping outside, Ken introduces himself.

"Hi. I'm Ken."

"Hello. I am Dave. What door needs fixing?"

"Let me show you." Ken starts to head round to the back of the house. "Right back here,"

The repair guy looks the door over and shakes his head up and down. "Pretty easy fix. I should have this done in 30 minutes."

"Just knock on the door when you are done." Knowing people hate it when someone looks over their shoulder, Ken excuses himself and goes back into the house.

This is great news for Ken. Being late to work is not something Ken enjoys. Raised that 'being on time is being successful,' it still reverberates in his mind, though he always questioned that saying when his dad repeated it.

Automatically Ken goes over to his chair and sits back down. The news was now reporting the weather and traffic. How quickly the news moves on to the next story. Ken questions himself if he could find out more information on the kid. Ken remembers that he has the officer's card. Pulling it from his pocket, he puts the number into his phone and hits the dial.

Just after 2 rings, the officer answers. "Officer Ellis. How may I help you?"

"Hi. This is Ken Hines. I am calling about the break-in last night at 6352 Shal...

Cutting off Ken in the middle of his sentence, the officer interrupts. "Yes. How can I help you."

Ken could feel the irritation rising in him but decided to be nice. "I was wondering about the young man they took into custody. Is there bail? Does he need anything?"

"He will have to return for his arraignment next Tuesday. He has been sent home in the custody of his mother." Theo officer explains.

The information was a little surprising to Ken, but he was also comforted by knowing the young man was not in jail right now. "Is there anything I can do for him?" Ken knew it was kind of a strange question. He wasn't sure how to ask if he could help the young man outside of bail fees.

The officer wasn't sure how to answer the question either. "Mr. Hill is back home with his siblings and mother. I am not sure what you could do for him."

"No, dad?"

"Dad has not been in the scene for a long time." The officer replies.

"Did you know Mr. Hill before last night?" Ken asks.

"He and some of his friends are known to the police at this station."

Ken wants to know more. "Meaning he has been in trouble before?"

The officer gives Ken a little bit about the background on the mischief Cody Hill and his friends have caused over the years. He explains how many young men in his neighborhood either do not have a dad at home or parents who are not truly present.

"Can I ask where the young man lives?"

"As he is a minor, I cannot give you the exact address," the officer hesitates. Then he continues, "You might venture over to Shadow Drive, about two minutes away from your house by car. Look for a dark green home on the street."

Jotting down the information, Ken thanks the officer and hangs up the phone. The timing was perfect as the repairman knocks on the front door. Checking the back door, Ken was pleased with his work. Paying the bill via his phone, the driver takes off. Ken could now head into work.

Work has been a place where he dives into his skills and where he can let himself forget about his troubles for a few hours every day. Unlike his co-workers, Ken does not find joy on Friday nights. To him, it meant forty-eight hours to get through on his own before he would return. He has never shared that secret depression with anyone. It's his silent torture he felt was due him.

Ken has never been fond of drawing attention to himself. Often women found themselves attracted to his quiet disposition. Many women seem to need to fix him, but he doesn't want to fix it. His past was his present. He had stopped looking into the future a few years ago. The future brings hope, and Ken isn't interested in being a hopeful man right now.

Getting into the office, Ken throws himself into his work. Architecture has always been a passion of his. Bringing life and beauty to commercial buildings was something he loved. He and his wife always dreamt about him designing a house for their retirement. She wanted an especially large kitchen since she loved to cook. He wanted a study to frame some of his work to show off to house guests. He no longer held that dream. It died a couple of years earlier.

Today he was completing a new library design with a nice atrium. He wants the feeling of being outside while patrons read or work inside. He designed the building with many windows and foliage to bring natural light and nature. The interior was of a light wood design, giving the library a more home-like feel. Kenneth Hines was known for the beauty he included in every building he designed. Many high-profile companies had sought him out for years, especially once he started winning awards for his work.

A reminder pops up on his computer for an upcoming meeting. He welcomes the break and starts to head into the conference room. Everything in this building is of a modern design and up to date. Ken has always loved the waterfall in the lobby and often takes that route to the large meeting room just to hear its sounds. As the water trickles down the fountain into the pond below, it makes nice comforting sounds. Ken had thought about buying himself a desk fountain but never did. Keeping it filled with water would just be another chore he would forget to do.

Opening the large conference glass door, he steps into the room. The podium was already set up at the far end of the room. Black leather chairs are all spaced evenly around the table and pushed in. Ken decides he would sit near the back, facing the large picture windows to the south side of the building. He prefers the view overlooking back into the office from the other side. The large mahogany oblong table filled most of the room. Pads of paper with pens and small clear glasses were poised in front of each chair. Two pitchers of water were in the table's center at both ends.

Ken helps himself by pouring water into his glass and sits down in his preferred chair. The cool water was refreshing. He says his hellos as other executive managers enter the room and take their seats.

Then, a young lady Ken does not recognize walks in. She is sharply dressed in a black suit, with a beautiful aqua-colored blouse. She is wearing a multi-colored dragonfly lapel pin. Her eyes are a gorgeous brown color made up of multiple shades. Placing her water bottle on the podium, Ken realizes she is today's guest speaker.

Rarely did guest speakers come into the office. Most of the time, the conference room was used to pitch clients new building designs. It was nice not to be the person at the podium today. He could just sit back and listen.

It was time to start. The young woman takes her place at the front podium, takes a sip of water, and begins to speak.

"Hello. My name is Adelle Rayne. I am the Executive Director and Founder of the Greater Lives Foundation. We understand your company chooses a charity annually to help support those in need during the holiday season. We appreciate you choosing our foundation this year. I will take you through a short presentation and open it up for questions. Sound good?"

Adelle notices Ken. His dark hair and blue eyes, like warm pools of light, drew her attention to him. As she speaks, she finds herself returning to him and his eyes. She senses that he has a heart of gold, but she can also feel pain radiating from him.

Most people at the table nod in agreement to Adelle's question. She jumps right in and starts the presentation. It was a lively presentation about helping underprivileged people in your community. The presentation speaks to the needs of the homeless and less fortunate. Ken found some of her suggestions interesting.

"Many people need basic items such as coats, socks, and underclothes. These are items that are in high demand. Homeless people could use blankets and food and shelter when possible." She goes on to explain how they ask for different items from various companies to ensure they do not receive a lot of the same items and to ensure they have a variety of certain items that are requested most often. "This process helps us have a little more control over all donations."

Participating in these events gives Ken a good feeling of giving back to those in need, though it has always been more out of a need for action rather than compassion or empathy.

Adelle begins to walk around the room, handing out her business card to all the attending executives. She had already taken the time to write down the items his firm had agreed to contribute this year on the back of the cards. They had all agreed-on supplying sleeping bags as well as used coats. The firm would send the company a memo for all willing to participate.

As she approached Ken, she made sure to talk to him. "Here is my card. The items your firm has agreed upon are written on the back. Please call me if you have any questions." Making eye contact, Ken acknowledges her words.

"Thank you, will do."

It all seems so familiar and routine. There were no surprises here today. The company makes these contributions every year. Ken always trips to the local department store with camping equipment and buys sleeping bags for the homeless. It was his way of giving back, and he loved to give more than he expected. He has a reputation for contributing the most every year. It is an easy way for Ken to give back. No real commitment. The gesture soothed him.

The workday was almost over. He starts to pack up his desk to head home. But before he turns off his computer, he has had one thought on his mind all day, *Where is Shadow Drive?*

Ken selects the street name in a map program and hits the search button. He quickly realizes he needs a little more information to narrow the search. Going back, he enters his city and state information and hits the enter button again.

There are two Shadow Drives near his house. They both were closer than he thought based on the description the officer had given him. He notices that, in truth, it was the same street, but railroad tracks separate the street into two different parts of town. Analyzing the map a little closer, he figures that his best bet would be the lower part of the street closer to the scantier part of town.

Making a mental note of the directions, Ken decides to divert his drive home to check out the street and the dark green house. His mind was slightly overdriven with thoughts about the young Mr. Hill. *Was it better to live what many consider a privileged life and die than to be a troubled young man?* Ken could not answer that question. He had not lived a sheltered life at all. But he also had not experienced much poverty. His family has always had food on the table, both parents, and a roof over their heads. Nothing had been handed to them, but there weren't a lot of obstacles in his way.

His thoughts were interrupted as he caught himself almost making an automatic turn on Walnut Road, his normal way home. Stopping himself from making the turn, he heads straight for the next two lights before making a left turn onto Shadow Drive. Slowing down, he looks at all the houses on the street. Ken starts to notice most of the houses deteriorate. Quite a few lawns have weeds or just dead grass. The cars are beaten up, and all older model vehicles, some with dents or fading paint. There are some well-kept homes, but the ratio is not in their favor.

Children play on the street. Soccer seems to be their favorite sport. A couple of boys are hanging out with their skateboards and scooters. They check out Ken and his car as he drives by. He realizes he probably sticks out since he has never been seen here. He laughs a little. His somewhat fancy car is a dead giveaway.

Looking a little ahead of his car, he catches a glimpse of a dark green house. It was small and in need of a good paint job. Pulling over to the opposite side of the street, he parks his car two doors down as he focuses on the children playing in the yard. It seems that the young Mr. Hill may have other siblings. Not that Ken believes they all belong to the family there, but at least one must.

The children are laughing and running after each another. It seemed to be some homemade kind of tag they were playing. However, the young man that lived in this house was nowhere in sight.

Becoming intrigued by their play, Ken watches them intently.

Knock, knock, knock, suddenly was heard on his passenger side window. It is a young black boy, and he is holding a football. His bright striped shirt brings a smile to Ken's face, as he remembers having one just like it when he was growing up.

Clicking on the car window button, he draws the window down halfway.

"Hello," Ken says, curious as to what the child will say. He was pretty sure it was going to be *Who are you?* Ken was not ready for the question the young man was about to ask.

With a confidence of a horse on the run, the boy boldly makes his request known. "Can you show me how to throw a football Mister, please?"

Slightly in shock, Ken looks back down the street. There was one thing missing. Men. Fathers. *Were they all at work? Wouldn't they be coming home now?* As he turns to answer the boy, the young man continues. "I don't have a dad or big brother to teach me. Will you?"

How could Ken refuse such a bold request? "Sure."

Turning off his car and stepping out, Ken felt unsure of what he was doing. No matter who made it, there was no way he would refuse such a request. Approaching the young man, he introduces himself.

"I'm Ken."

"I'm Mykel. M-Y-K-E-L"

"Hello, Mykel. Do you know how to hold the ball to throw it?"

Mykel shakes his head no as he hands the football over to Ken. Ken tosses the ball over to Mykel. Mykel, in return, tosses the ball back. It was almost like an underhand toss and not a pass at all.

Right away, Ken begins his instruction and shows the young man where to place his hand and fingers on the ball to throw it. "Okay, you need to grip the ball like this. Your index finger should be over a seam, and your thumb and index fingers should make an "L" shape. See that?" Showing Mykel his hand with the ball.

"Next, you must position yourself facing about 90 degrees from your target. Since you throw with your right hand, turn to the right. Don't hold the ball too tight. Turn your pivot foot opposite your throwing arm so that it's pointing toward your target. Keep your eyes on the target." Ken demonstrates the position.

Continuing, and knowing he was giving Mykel a lot of information at once, he slows his speech down. "The ball and arm go near your ear. Make sure it is not moving with your other hand like this. Then wind back like this. Throw in a half-circular motion and quickly swing your throwing arms forward in an arc. Make sure to release the ball midway. "

Ken sends the ball back to Mykel. Catching the ball, Mykel steps up to put all the new notes into practice. He holds the ball as best as he can.

His hands are smaller than Ken's, but he does pretty well.

"Yes, you have it. Now position your body facing as I showed you." Mykel shifts his stance a little to be standing correctly. Winding back, he tosses his first pass.

"Much better." Ken throws the ball back to Mykel to mimic the pattern.

"Okay, Mykel. Toss it over here."

The toss was good, but Ken knew he would have to tackle posture and the footing stance a little more. After instructing Mykel for another 5 minutes, a great toss game takes place. Feeling pride in the young man's achievements, Ken thought about the powerful feeling surging in his body at that moment. It felt exceptional. He knew he was smiling, and he was enjoying himself. It had been quite some time since he had the giggles in his stomach.

His stone-cold heart was beginning to melt. Just like ice, it starts with a few cracks.

While tossing the ball back and forth, Ken never noticed that young Hill had stepped out to his front porch and began to watch the two at play. He sat down on the steps to his house and stared as he wished he could join them. He would not be as bold as Mykel, but that was about to change. Mr. Hill did not recognize Ken as the man whose house he broke into just a few nights earlier. He was too frightened to remember much about that night other than a gun being pointed at him and his friend dying.

CHAPTER THREE

There is newfound energy in Ken's step. Getting home just after dark, he heads directly for his kitchen. Tonight, he was going to whip up a meal for himself. He took lamb chops out of the freezer to let them thaw a little. Rummaging through his refrigerator, he found some good asparagus. He also knew he had an instant rice medley he could microwave. He starts cooking.

The fragrance of the meat filled the house. He pulls out a nice plate and sets the table as it simmers. For months now, he started a pattern of picking up dinner on the way home from work. Tonight, he was changing it up.

Placing the lamb on the right side of the plate, he then positions his sautéed asparagus to the left before adding a nice mound of the medley to the plate. He could hardly wait to dive in. But one thing was missing, a nice red wine. Popping the cork for a bottle from his small wine rack, he pours the wine into his glass and brings it to the table.

He places his napkin across his lap as if in a fancy restaurant and digs in. The lamb cut like butter as the juices flowed out. The taste that hits his tongue fills his senses. He chews slowly, savoring each bite. His favorite meal for a very successful day.

Just finishing the last bite, Ken leans back in the chair, holding his wine. He had at least two sips left. Taking in the house, Ken realizes how dark it appears. He decided that maybe it was time to do something about it. It wouldn't be tonight, though, as he had plans to go upstairs and sleep in his bed.

Morning always came soon enough. It was the first time he had slept in his bed in months, and he realized the normal aches and pains of sleeping in a lounge chair were not present. He feels a little younger somehow. Maybe because of the lack of discomfort he felt this morning, or maybe the game of tossing a football brought back youthful memories. It didn't matter why; Ken was taking it all in.

Jumping into the warm, steamy shower, Ken spends a few extra minutes letting the warm water wash over his tight skin. The soap suds roll off his skin as he runs the washrag over every inch of his body. He has already decided to visit Shadow Drive again tonight.

Heading off to work, Ken is back in his rhythm. He already knows it will feel like a long day since he plans to sneak out a little early to see if he can find Mykel again. He would check his cell phone clock all day, waiting for the day to end. He hoped he would not be disappointed, but they had not made arrangements to meet again after Mykel had been called into the house for dinner.

Finally, the hour came, and Ken made it through the workday. He heads out of the office a little early. He heads to Shadow Drive, jumping into his car after placing his computer in his trunk. Pulling up two doors down from the dark greenhouse, he parks on the opposite side of the street again, in front of Mykel's house, just like the day before. Looking around, Ken didn't see Mykel. Other children played outside, but Ken did not feel comfortable approaching them.

No Mykel. An hour had passed. Ken begins to feel a little depressed as he hears a knock on his passenger window. It was Mykel, but this time he was not alone. Mykel had two friends with him.

Ken bounces out of the car and walks over to where they are standing. "Hello, Mykel. And who are these fine gentlemen?"

The boys giggle. None of them have ever been called that before. They were not sure what to make of it. "This is Conrad, and this is Sammie." The boys glared at Ken, not knowing what to do next. Proper etiquette 101 was about to commence.

"Hello, Mr. Conrad. It is a pleasure to meet you." Ken extends his hand as they shake.

"Mr. Sammie. A pleasure to meet you as well." Ken repeats the gesture. Turning his attention to Mykel. "Did you practice last night?"

"No. It was too dark to go outside, and my mom won't let us play ball in the house." Ken chuckles a little at that.

"So, are you men ready to play a little ball toss then?" Ken asks. The boys were immediately excited. They all respond with an enthusiastic yes.

"Okay. Let's all take positions about ten feet from each other. Mykel, will you do the honors and throw the first ball?"

Staying on the front lawn area, the boys all stand equally apart. Mykel sends out the first toss toward Ken. It was a little short, but Ken was ready for it. Taking the ball in his hand, he gives a little refresher course for Mykel, designed for the other two boys. Ken didn't know if any of them had the chance to play ball.

Sammie is a young white boy, approximately age 11. He has dark hair and a medium build, while

Conrad has darker skin but isn't fully black. When Ken was waiting to see if Mykel would show up, he noticed some of the other occupants of the street. The area has a wide population of various people. Poverty here was not confined.

Taking a second to look around between throws, Ken notices Cody sitting on the steps to his house. "Mykel, do you know that young man across the street?"

Mykel looks to see who Ken is referring to and recognizes Cody. "Yeah. That's Cody"

"Is he a friend of yours?" Ken asks.

"Not really. He is a little older. I doubt he wants to hang with kids like me?"

Ken was not sure exactly what Mykel was saying. "Like you?"

"Yea. No boys his age want to hang with kids our age."

Ken wasn't sure how true that was. "Would you mind if I invite him to practice with us?

Mykel shrugs his shoulders up. "Go ahead. He will say no."

Ken tosses the ball back over to Conrad and heads towards Cody. "Excuse me. Do you want to join in on the practice?"

Sitting still for a few moments, Ken could tell Cody was weighing his options. Finally, he stands up and starts to head toward Ken. Ken turns to head back to the other boys as Cody follows. Now that there are five of them, they shift their locations to keep extra distance between them.

Conrad immediately tosses the ball to Cody. He catches it and throws it to Sammie. They all continued taking turns until it was dusk. They all said their goodbyes. Once again, Mykel asks Ken, "Can you come tomorrow?"

"Sure can."

Ken knew that a person's life could hinge on a single instant. The loss of his family was one such moment. The tapping on his car window was another one. But this time, Ken wasn't conscious of all that was taking place inside himself. He did know it felt good.

CHAPTER FOUR

The nightly visits to Shadow Drive and playing ball with the young men change Ken's life. Their conversations are much more than just football. It seems the boys have begun talking to Ken like a father figure. Ken remembers the previous night's conversation.

"Why are you not sleeping well at night?" Ken asked Mykel.

"I worry."

"Worry about what? Grades? Girls?" Ken questioned.

"My mom. She works hard."

"All parents work hard for their children. They try their best." Ken explained. He went on to talk about

a parent's love for their child. Ken decided to leave out that not all parents are the same.

Work was almost becoming an afterthought. His mind seems to stay on the young men and how he could help them. He had decided that the boys needed an adventure. Something full of fun.

Ken was excited about spending quality time with the neighborhood children. Ken got the crazy idea that the children would have a great time if he could take all of the young men to an upcoming NFL game. He wasn't sure, but he figured that probably none of them had ever been to one. Ken had taken his young son a couple of years ago.

After checking with Mykel's mother, who asked a few other neighborhood parents, Ken got the okay to arrange a day at the stadium. A couple of other adults would chaperone the day with Ken and the children. Ken would pay for it all. Once he got the okay, he bought several seats at the fifty-yard line, about 15 rows up.

Renting a van, Ken drives up to Mykel's house and honks the horn. The children all barrel out of the house and run to the van's side door. After closing the van's side door, Conner's father walks out and gets into the passenger seat.

"Everyone in a seat and seat belts on, please." The boys laugh and wiggle around as they all find their belts and click them. Excited boys can be loud, but the noise level does not bother Ken. It is a joyous sound to Ken, something he misses dearly.

Once parked at the stadium, the boys walk briskly to their seats. They were ready for cheering, yelling, and just being crazy. The vendors walk the aisles selling their wares. Ken buys each boy a hotdog and a drink. Later he would make sure they each got to catch a flying bag of peanuts. No football experience is complete unless you catch hot roasted peanuts from a few rows away.

Rooting for the home team, the boys jump from their seats and dance after each touchdown. They boo and hiss at any call they don't like from the refs. Ken is grateful that everyone near them also has children doing the same things. No one complains. The infectious joy seems to pump up all the children sitting near them.

The ride back home is quite the opposite of the ride out. The boys are slumped over, sleeping. The full day has taken a toll on all of them.

"This was such a fantastic time out. I don't know how to thank you." Conner's dad expresses.

"You are welcome. It was fun for me too." Ken replies.

"You are single? Is that right?" Conner's dad asks.

"Single? No." Pausing for a second before he continues, Ken tries to explain in as few words as possible and with deep sincerity, "I am a widow. Lost my child too." Painfully Ken frowns.

The topic was not going well. "Sorry to hear that." Connor's dad realizes his mistake and does not know how to recover from it. Though Ken waits for more conversation, instead, everyone lapses into silence. Ken starts staring forward at the highway as headlights fly past them from the opposite direction.

Once back home, the parents come out to collect their children, each thanking Ken as they share how much they appreciate him taking them for the day. Ken knows the next morning would bring the children sharing their stories about the day. But now, they were all heading off to bed.

Ken would not be doing the same. He could not help wondering what other things the young men had not experienced. What things did he take for granted in his own life growing up? Football was one thing. It can teach courage, teamwork, commitment, and communication about how to handle defeat or loss. Ken knows he can teach them these skills if they let him continue. But there is a lot more to life and a lot more to becoming a man.

The day had been great fun for Ken. He could not shake the feeling there was much more he could do. He also wondered about Conner's dad.

Why hadn't he ever taken Connor to a game? What was he missing? He knows their fight is to survive. Food on the table is a higher commitment than sporting events. Ken wonders if there is something more.

As he replays the day in his head, lightning strikes. The football tickets cost, food, parking, all round out to about one thousand seven hundred dollars for four hours of fun and excitement. Most likely something many of these families cannot afford.

The basics to get by having to be a priority. Choices have to be made. Ken remembers back to his childhood. His parents were not wealthy by any means. His parents gave up a lot for him to play sports. His mother hardly ever bought new clothes. His dad would go to work wearing the same suit almost every day. Ken had worked hard to get great grades in the hope of getting a scholarship, which he was eventually awarded. However, it did not cover all his college expenses. His parents continued to make sacrifices for him to have a better life.

It wasn't until he started his career and money started coming in that he could repay his parents for all they had done for him. The first thing he bought them was a car because their car was on its last legs. They had driven it into the ground.

He moved out of their neighborhood, much like Cody's and Mykel's community. When he could, he helped his parents retire closer to him and his family and got his dad to retire. Ken misses his parents as much as he does his own family. The loss of everyone around him has given Ken the feeling of being alone in the world.

CHAPTER FIVE

It was late. It felt like everyone in the world was sleeping except Ken. He found himself sitting in a chair in his late son's room thinking, going through memories of his hopes and plans that his son would out succeed in his accomplishments. His dreams were trickling back into his mind. His heart was melting.

The bedroom set was designed for racing cars. His dresser has a painted racetrack on it. His bedspread has various racing cars in red, black, and dark blue, with matching curtains. A small bookshelf held a couple of little trophies from racing model cars. The bedroom was designed as a city, complete with streets.

A grin starts to break out on Ken's face as he recalls painting the bedroom walls of the room with his son. Since his son was not an artist nor very tall, he was tasked with painting the grass at the foot of the wall while Ken painted checkered flags higher up, closer to the ceiling.

It had been a long time since Ken allowed these memories to surface. The pain that comes with them is often overwhelming. He feels as if he is drowning in emotion without the ability to surface to catch a breath.

Pressure around his throat begins to make it hard to breathe. Tears begin to fall as Ken is curled up on his son's floor, moaning.

"I want you back," Ken screams. "Come back." He begins to rock back and forth a little.

Several minutes go by before Ken returns his breath as he reaches for a tissue. He knows he has to get out of the room immediately. His emotions are tearing him apart. At once, he heads to his bathroom and splashes water on his face. Placing both hands on each side of the sink, he drops his head as his mind yells at him as to why he let himself feel all that pain.

Slowly lifting his head, Ken catches a glimpse of himself in the mirror. His eyes were red and swollen, and he looked like hell. He grabs the towel from the rack and quickly dabs his face to remove the excess water. He looks away from the mirror that reflects his truth and heads downstairs.

Everything was quiet. You could hear the proverbial pin hit the ground. It was several minutes before Ken heard a sound. It was his phone.

"Hello." Ken wondered who would be calling him at this hour.

A strong voice came over the phone. "Hello, Mr. Hines. This is Officer Ellis. I hope I didn't wake you."

Ken's mind raced as he wondered why the officer would be calling him now. "No, you didn't. I am up. How can I help you?" What could the officer need now, he questions?

"Your attendance for the upcoming scheduled court date for Cody Hill will no longer be necessary."

Wow, Ken could believe what he was hearing. Had Cody decided to plead guilty after all?

"Thanks for letting me know. Is he pleading guilty?" Ken asks.

"Sorry, Mr. Hines. He is dead," the officer states as mere fact. The words do not fully penetrate Ken's mind. Did the officer say he was dead? He had just played ball with him earlier that week. With his brain still spinning, Ken needs help understanding.

"Dead? How? What happen...." Ken trails off as his own words echo in his mind. He has heard these words too many times in his own life. To hear them again was devastating. Ken's world was crushing in on him again.

The news was seismic to Ken. The concrete below his house flooring was turning to shift sand. Life was in the process of gobbling him up yet again. *When would all this death stop?*

"He and a couple of buddies broke into a store. As they hastily left on their bikes, Cody was hit by a truck. As he ran from the scene, the driver never saw him as he darted between two parked cars. He was dead on impact."

Ken was silent as the officer added one more thought. "These streets are not for the timid. Young men grow up quickly to survive."

The words rang in Ken's ears. It deafens his thoughts and crushes his spirit. In a whisper, Ken tells the officer, "Thank you for notifying me, officer." Ken eases his cell phone down to the table.

Another loss leaves Ken wondering how life can be so cruel. The young man had his whole life ahead of him. He was the reason he found Shadow Drive in the first place. Ken wants to sit in his old chair and stare blindly at the TV. His old habit sounds like comfort to him right now. But was it?

That would be going backward for Ken. He knew it. He felt it. Ken averts his eyes from his mirror as he goes upstairs to get ready for bed. He knows if he looks at his reflection now, his eyes will reveal the hard truth of his pain. They would reveal his anguish, and he would have to accept it.

CHAPTER SIX

Ken sits silently with his pencil stilled. He was not marking the building layout he was supposed to be reviewing. Every architect has their preference for making revisions. Ken loved the old-school way of using a pencil. He could draw lines with very light strokes before deciding if he agrees with his observation of the suggested loose change. If not, he could simply erase it and start again.

One thought was bouncing around in his mind. Life was not that simple. He could not erase the pain in his life and just transform who he is. Cody Hill could not erase his mistakes and start over again. Making adjustments in life is not that easy.

As she walks through the halls, Adelle sees Ken staring at a large paper page. She assumes it was planned for a project, but that would be an educated guess. She stops at the doorway to his office and studies him for a few seconds. Not wanting to be discovered staring, she says, "Hello."

Looking over at where the hello came from, Ken sees Adelle.

"Hello. You are back."

"Yes. I dropped off the containers for the donations. How are you?" Adelle asks.

"Good. Do you have a moment? Please come in."

Entering further into the office, she comes closer to Ken. He continues. "I am wondering about other services your charity provides."

Adelle becomes curious. Wanting more conversation with Ken, Adelle welcomes any questions he may have. Her hopes of getting to know him better could stem from what he is asking her. "What kind of services?"

"Helping people in need with homes but not a lot of money."

More than happy to get involved, but Adelle still

is not sure what Ken is thinking. "Is there something you have in mind?"

Ken knows he is not making a lot of sense. Maybe starting over would be a good idea. "I met a young man recently. I know his family can't afford much. They can't even afford to have him in sports because gear costs so much. I took him and a few friends to their first NFL game. They had great fun. It was a great experience for them. I am wondering if your organization does anything like that for families."

Ken realizes he was talking pretty fast. Adelle could not have gotten in a single word if she wanted to. "Something like that?" he adds.

Adelle smiles. His excitement is making him even cuter than she already sees him as. His passion for this young man is certainly honorable.

Feeling as if he was making a fool, he makes the mistake of continuing in his intense and direct manner. "I know that NFL games are unnecessary in life, but things like this help round out a life. It can give a young person enjoyment and excitement in everyday life."

Now Ken feels even sillier. He abruptly stops speaking.

Listening to every word that Ken spoke, Adelle took it all in. She knows instantly that there must be a story behind what Ken is attempting to say. Since he had not elaborated on it, the passion behind the words stirred something within her.

Ken waits. He feels her gaze upon him, and for the first moment, he sees her. They stand eye to eye. His thoughts of embarrassment were washing away as her unblinking eyes were focused solely on him. After a silence, she spoke.

"Yes, we help people in need with all sorts of projects. We have everything from programs that help feed people to programs that help mothers in need with newborns. And yes, we take children to events to expand their cultural awareness."

Ken waits for Adelle to continue, but instead, the silence resumes. He didn't know what she was expecting. "Sorry. I don't even know where to start. What would be our next step?"

Adelle found comfort in the word "our" and

repeated it clearly in the next words she spoke. "Our next step is to determine what we want to do for these children...."

Ken interrupts quickly. "Families." Nodding in agreement, Adelle continues backing up her last few words. "... what exactly we want to do for these families and when we want to do it. Do you have any ideas?"

Being someone driven by taking an idea and creating something out of nothing, Ken was a little amazed at the fact he was somewhat lost in the moment. "No, not really. Not yet." He glances at her.

"I would be happy to meet up with you again next week to see if any ideas have come your way."

"That would be great. I can try to figure out what they need." As the air conditioner kicks back on, a whiff of her light perfume makes him smile a bit at its aroma. His thoughts become tangled up in her beauty instead of his plans. Her skin was fair, soft and perfect. Her eyes are golden brown. They looked to him like deep Manuka honey. Her hair is dark and wavy and fell just right on her shoulders.

"Make sure it is something you are passionate about. The word 'need' makes it seem more like an obligation than what I hear you saying." Adelle cautions. "Figure out what you want to give them. Maybe furnish them, meaning you might want to provide a fun event more than pay their bills."

His gaze broke off as he knew he had feelings inside him that he had not felt for some time. A slight embarrassment arose in his gut as he was sure Adelle could read his mind.

"Thank you. I will take that under consideration." Heading to his desk calendar, he flips a couple of pages. "How is next Wednesday for you? Maybe over lunch?" he said, hoping he was much more subtle than he felt he was being.

Scrolling across her phone for a minute, she responded, "That would be perfect. Do you have a place in mind?"

"I can call you Tuesday to make sure we are still on, and I will suggest a place then. How does that sound?"

"Perfect. I will be looking forward to it."

He could not resist looking at her once more as she headed out his office door. Her stride was one of confidence, and her shape was perfect. She immediately headed to the right once outside his door. He shook his head in almost disgust. Speaking to himself, "What are you a friggin' high school boy?"

Adelle couldn't wait to call her friend Jan. She had told her about Ken the day of the presentation. She told Jan about her desire to get to know him better. Jan had encouraged her to step outside her comfort zone and make the first move. Adelle had promised she would at least say hi to him and leave her card. She is excited that she did what she said. She was even more amazed that Ken was already thinking about talking with her.

She didn't even make it back to her car before dialing Jan.

"How did it go?" Jan answers the phone. "Did you keep your promise?"

"I did. He is so nice. He wants to do some kind

of event for some families and wants my help." Adelle explains.

"That is great news. We should celebrate. Meet me at The Explorer Bar. Say 5 pm," Jan offers.

"How about in 15 minutes?" Adelle says back.

"On my way."

Adelle wants to tell Jan every detail of the conversation and how she felt, and hopefully, Jan will help her figure out how to handle whatever is next. Jan is always willing to offer up advice.

CHAPTER SEVEN

The sun had rose and fell before Ken found himself back on Shadow Drive. Just as he reaches Mykel's house, he sees the young man sitting on the second stair leading to his front porch. His head is hanging down with both hands holding his head in place. As he parks his car, Ken feels dread in the pit of his stomach.

Approaching Mykel, he goes right for his confession. "Mykel, I am so sorry I couldn't make it yesterday. I don't know how to get a hold of you to let you know."

"Oh, hello, Mr. Hines," Mykel mutters. "It's okay. I don't expect you here every day." Ken felt a little reassured but didn't know why Mykel appeared so gloomy. Sitting on the same step right next to the young man, he starts questioning him.

"Is something wrong? Is your family okay?"

"Yeah, they are okay."

Ken remembers that the boy across the street, Cody, had passed away, and maybe that fact has saddened Mykel. "Are you upset about losing your friend from across the street?" Ken asks. Mykel does not respond.

Maybe just sitting quietly for a while would coax Mykel into talking. Ken prepares to be there for a little while before a new conversation might happen. However, Mykel surprises Ken when he starts talking.

"I failed my spelling test today. I don't want to disappoint my mom again. I studied. I did."

"I believe you, Mykel."

"I just can't keep the words straight in my head. I'm stupid."

"No. You are not stupid. You picked up on football faster than any other young man I have taught."

"You're just saying that."

"Ha. That's kind of funny. In my adult world,

people tell me I am too honest."

Mykel lifts his head and quickly studies Ken's face for any telltale signs of a mistruth. "Really?"

"Really."

"Do you want me to help you study?"

"You would do that?"

"Sure. Maybe we can connect some of what you are learning to football. Want to try?" Mykel shrugs his shoulder as if to say why not. "Give me a word you had to spell today that you messed up on."

"Hmm, the word that means speaking." Ken can tell that Mykel is searching for the word. "Odd... odd-a."

"Audible?"

"Yes, that's it."

"That's perfect. Grab your football and get on the grass." Mykel jumps up from the steps and heads to the far side of the yard.

"Throw me the ball," Ken commands. Mykel obeys and gives the ball a great toss. "Bring it in." Ken motions for Mykel to step in closer. "Before each play, you see the team gather like this."

They both pretend to huddle. "So, what is happening when they do this?"

"The quarterback is telling them what to do."

"Right. He is giving them the play." Standing up, Ken steps back. "What happens next?"

Mykel was beaming as he knew all the answers. "They go to their positions, and he gives them the signal."

"Right, snap on three. What happens when the Quarterback sees a player on the opposing side change location on the field and knows the play won't work?"

"He changes the play?"

"Right again. Each team has coded. A quarterback calls out the codes for the play he is changing it to. That is audible in football." Something clicks for Mykel. He could easily associate the word with the football term.

"So, let's think of some way you can associate it

with spelling it."

"I don't understand."

"Aud-i-ball. How do you listen to your favorite music?"

"My phone."

"Therefore, your phone is an audio system, right?"

"Yeah."

"Calling a ball change out load is hyphened as Audi – drop the o- ball. A."

"Wait, Wait... A-U-D-I...." Pausing for a slight second as Mykel knew it was not spelled B-A-L-L. "...B... L.E."

"Correct!! Now give me your best touchdown dance."

Mykel laughs. Spiking the ball to the ground, he wiggles and dances. Ken joins in and tries to mimic Mykel. Ken knew they must look ridiculous, but he could care less.

They take on a couple more words before it is total dusk, and Mykel would have to go inside.

"Mykel, I want you to do something for me tomorrow."

"Okay. What?"

"I want you to ask your teacher to tell you these five words we worked on tonight and let you spell them without writing them down. Can you do that?"

"I can."

"Do you promise?"

"Sure. But I don't know that she cares."

"Do it anyways. And if she doesn't help you, start spelling the words out loud and make sure she hears you. I will ask for a full report tomorrow."

Ken knew in his heart that if Mykel returned tomorrow to tell him the teacher didn't care, he would be heading to that school in the morning.

Arriving home, Ken knew his life was roaring down a road he had never seen coming. For the past couple of years, he had positioned himself in a place of constant sadness that had become comfortable. Misery was a friend he had grown to know well and, at times, did not want to see go. Now, he was being pursued by something thundering into his life, and he could not stop it. He knows without question fate was at his front door.

Mykel was grinning all the way home. He couldn't wait to tell his mom the news. He burst into his house as if it were on fire and was there to rescue the family. "Mom! MOM!" His voice increases in pitch. "Mom, are you home?"

"Yes, dear. What's wrong?" Mykel pulls out a paper from behind his back. In the top left-hand corner, was a giant red letter "A" with a plus sign behind it. He had passed his spelling test.

"Great job, son." His mother hugged him, picking him off the ground and swinging him in a giant circle.

He could hardly wait for Ken to show up. He was so excited.

CHAPTER EIGHT

Looking at his shoes, Ken was a little baffled that they still held a shine since he had not worn them for over 2 years. His black slacks hit the shoe tops perfectly. Double checking his black jacket to ensure there was no lint, he took the lint brush over it one more time before sliding it over his solid black shirt and tie.

It was a day that he had experienced before. This time he wasn't the focus of the ceremony but a bystander. Entering the church, Ken slides into the last pew. The church is small. It has one stained-glass window, and a basic wooden cross with a colorful piece of silk draped over it. Several rows of old wooden pews that show a lot of wear and tear offer parishioners an uncomfortable place to sit.

Various people were taking turns talking about

their memories of Cody. The anecdotes made the young man out to be a saint. *Why hash over anything bad since the person isn't here to defend himself* Ken reasons with himself.

As the service ends, Ken continues to hang out in the back of the church, averting his face from others as often as he can. As all the attendees leave and head outside, the preacher notices Ken hanging in the back and walks over to him.

"Hello. Did you know Cody?"

Ken turns to face him. "Yes."

"How do you know him?"

Ken loves the idea that the preacher refers to Cody as still alive. "Oh, he broke into my house a few weeks back."

The preacher gestures in acknowledgment. "He confessed to that."

"Are you allowed to tell me that?" Ken asks.

"Well, it seems not to be a secret. I thought you should know he had some remorse."

Ken wasn't that surprised. "I know. He was a great kid. I'm sure peer pressure played a part in it. A need to fit in."

"I agree. The neighborhood is full of it."

Correcting the preacher, Ken states the obvious. "It is peer pressure everywhere at this age. Not just here. It just manifests differently." The preacher knew Ken was right. His wisdom was not lost on him.

Continuing, Ken asked, "Was the funeral paid for? Does the family need anything?" Ken asks.

"Yes. The funeral is taken care of." Ken was happy to hear that news. Reaching out his hand, he shakes hands with the preacher. "Thank you."

Ken heads to the cemetery, a hundred feet behind the church. Before he can get out the door, he hears the preacher say something.

"Headstone. They are burying Cody with his brother."

Ken turns around and looks at the preacher. "Their decision?"

"Yes. His mother wants them together. They didn't have to pay for another plot, but it was the togetherness she wanted. No one wants to bury one son, let alone two. At least they can be together."

Ken had no idea that his brother had also died. It wasn't the right time to ask. Ken took it in as his heart sunk further. "Headstone?"

"They don't have money for a headstone."

"What do they cost?" Ken knew he had spent a couple of thousand dollars for his wife and child's headstone, but he could afford it. Worse is the fact he had thought it would lessen the pain, but it did the exact opposite.

"One hundred for a very basic plaque. Three for a small headstone and five hundred for an upright slate black granite."

Reaching into his pants pocket, Ken pulls out his money clip. Counting a few bills, Ken separates them from the clip and hands them to the preacher. "Make sure it is special." Having seen other children in the yard playing, Ken has one more question. "Are there more children in the family?"

"Yes, Cody has two more younger siblings. A sister and a younger brother."

"Thanks." Ken had been right. Two of the children he had seen playing in the yard were related. With that, Ken heads out of the church and joins the families at the grave site.

"You are a blessed young man." The pastor calls out after him.

Ken heard the words; however, he could not agree. If God blessed him, then why was his family dead? It couldn't be further from the truth.

Ken recognizes Conner's dad among the crowd while still keeping out of sight and in the background as much as possible since few knew him, and he didn't want to be the focus of anything. Ken did not want another person asking who he was. Being there was harder than Ken had imagined. Being at a cemetery was making him choke up. He was fighting back his tears and emotions to stay present. He was relieved to have something else to focus on as the preacher took his spot at the head of the grave and began to speak. His words were short and to the point.

As they lowered the casket into the grave, flowers were thrown on top of the casket. Memories were flooding back into Ken's head. The pain began surging back into his chest, and breathing became harder. Lowering his head, he squeezes his eyes to stop the tears from coming. Ken wipes his eyes with both hands before looking up just in time to see the preacher speaking with Cody's mother and pointing at him.

As if standing on a lazy Suzie, Ken spins on his heels and heads back to his car. He couldn't walk fast enough. He knows he never told the preacher that he wanted his donation to be kept anonymous so he could not be angry at him. Ken's emotions were getting the better of him. His thinking was anything but clear right now. He was not even sure he should be driving a car right now. He only knows he has to leave and go somewhere else and fast.

Ken did not recognize that Mykel's mother was also at the funeral. She had seen him. He did not know that a few days earlier, when he was sitting on the stairs in front of her house talking with Mykel, she had been standing at the screen door listening to every word. Any good mother would wonder why a grown man would hang out with her child. That day she knew Ken was a good man. What she doesn't know is his back story. She would have to correct that.

After getting home, Ken walks straight upstairs. Kicking off his shoes, he curls up on his son's bed and starts sobbing. All six feet of him go into the fetal position while slightly rocking back and forth. The sorrow envelops him completely. He can't stop. His emotions come flooding back as if the accident happened yesterday. He doesn't want to stop feeling the pain and sorrow. Preventing himself from wailing aloud was his only motive. He was afraid he could not control his volume. Struggling through it all, he eventually wears himself out and cries himself to sleep.

CHAPTER NINE

Thankfully, it has been a couple of days since the funeral, and Ken is feeling steady on his own feet. The emotional release a few days ago has lightened his mental load a little. He finds himself examining the drawing of the overall building look and feel he had been working on for the past couple of weeks. The professional building was sharp and with a low-risk factor like many buildings, Ken had designed in the last few years.

Unlike the buildings before this one, Ken studies the images repeatedly. What was missing? Any architect could design this building. Nothing screamed that this building was taking into account the natural surroundings. Nothing sends a message that someone wants to approach this building. Something was stirring in Ken.

Reaching behind him, he snatches up the pictures on the desk behind him. They are images of the empty lot this building will be constructed on. Some rolling hills will be behind the development. It will be located a few hundred yards from the main road, but not on top. And four large trees will have to be cut down.

Ken began to focus on the trees. *What if I use the trees in the actual design of the building?* He wonders. Create a building that includes trees. Maybe even create a waterfall and small pond where employees could lunch and take breaks. Alter the entrance from the freeway to the building with a fun, slightly winding road leading to the building with foliage along the way.

Starting over, Ken knows he only has until Friday to prepare his presentation. He has done it before, and Ken is determined to do it now. However, he would have to take a break in an hour as it is Wednesday, and he has a lunch date with Adelle.

As his watch alarm goes off, Ken already had

a good idea of redesigning the professional office and its space. Placing his pencil down, he grabs his small briefcase and heads out to meet Adelle. He still is unsure what exactly he has in mind for Mykel and his friends, but he has an idea.

Getting to the restaurant, he finds Adelle sitting patently in the guest area waiting for him.

"Am I late?" Ken chuckles, knowing he is five minutes early.

"Not at all. I put my name in if that's okay."

"That's great. Thank you. How are you today?" Ken asks.

"Busier than usual."

That comment sparks another question, but before Ken can ask, they both hear, "Adelle, the party of 2." Ken acknowledges the call by raising his hand. The host leads them to their table. Once seated and after they complete their drink orders, Ken jumps back in.

"You said you are busier than normal?"

"Companies feel an obligation now to give back

to their communities. It appears to be a part of their actual marketing strategy."

Ken understood those comments. "My company has been doing it for years without boasting about what we offer."

A huge grin appears on Adelle's face. "That is why I love working with your group of people. You guys seem so genuine. You're not just doing it as a fad."

As the server brought the iced teas, they both ordered some bread; they paused for a second as they took sips from their glasses.

"So, Ken, have you come up with any ideas?"

"I have. The other night I saw an old movie. A black and white film. Not even sure why I was watching it. Anyways, they showered children with toys and goodies for the holidays."

As Ken spoke, Adelle was fixated on his eyes. Describing what he had in mind made his eyes sparkle with excitement while his face showed a humble expression. She knows he wants to participate in something great but realizes he has no idea what he is doing. This innocence was drawing her in. His passion for the project was warming her heart.

Ken was still talking, "Maybe I should explain that my house was broken into a little while ago. The young man seemed to be going along under peer pressure to fit in with the cool boys. His dilemma broke my heart. The arresting officer gave me the area in which he lives. I went over there to see an entire community in hopes that maybe I could do something. Sound silly?"

Shaking her head to signal a no as she begins to speak. "It all starts somewhere. Everyone has their reason for getting involved."

Contemplating Adelle's words, Ken studies her for what he thinks is a split second. Her blouse was very feminine, with flowers and short ruffled sleeves. The V-neckline is flattering to her form. It is the confidence with which she speaks that captures Ken's thoughts. It is obvious to him that Adelle is both highly intelligent and passionate about what she does. He realizes he was looking at her intently and that she was watching him as well. Their eyes locked at that moment.

The food came to the table as if right on cue. Both use the break to take an instant to gather their thoughts. The joy of being with someone of the opposite sex penetrated his breathing ability. Not that Ken had never had these feelings before, but he was surprised to know they were still possible. He had never thought he would feel them again. Emotions were awakening in him. He thought they were long gone. He believed that these feelings of joy, love, and laughter died with his family. He was hoping Adelle would never ask the real question of him. *What was his real reason for getting involved?*

Changing the topic could be a surefire way to get further away from that question.

"When you are not working, what do you do for fun?" Ken asks Adelle.

"Oh. I love gardening, cooking, and sailplaning."

Almost choking on his food with the last note she dropped on him. "Sailplanes? A plane without an engine, right?"

"Yep."

"Isn't that dangerous?"

"Probably less than a plane with a heavy engine."

Adventurous too. Ken felt he was going down for the count. Adelle played back.

"And you? What do you do for fun?"

Ken had to think. It had been a while since he had had hobbies. Then he thought about Mykel. "I teach a couple of young boys how to play football and mentor them on their homework." Ken starts to worry after he responds that he leads her back to that question. Talking about the loss of his wife and child was not something he wanted to tackle today. His luck held out.

"Wow. That is awesome." Ken's answer warms Adelle's heart even more. She had been single for some time and, like Ken, had not thought about having someone else in her life. She, too, was getting a tugging feeling to want more.

"This is starting to feel like a date." Ken spouts off.

"Does it?" Adelle asks.

"Well, it does. At least the way I remember them being."

Adelle agrees and lets Ken know she doesn't go on many. "It's been a while for me too."

As they finished eating their lunch, they learned a little more about each other before turning the conversation back to what Ken wanted to accomplish, and Adelle knew she could help him. More importantly, she wants to help him.

"I can contact two other organizations and see if they want to get involved." Adelle offers.

"Perfect. I will contact a couple of companies I had as clients who loved my work and see if they want in on the action."

"Perfect. Let's regroup in two weeks." Adelle suggests.

"How about next week?" Ken interjects. He knew he did not want to wait two weeks to see her again. Letting out a little giggle, Adelle happily agrees.

Returning to the office after lunch, Ken finds himself with new vigor. Picking up his pencil, he begins to draw without stopping. He starts by placing the building around the trees with all glass atriums. He adds two more trees to a lunch area and a fountain that splashes into a brook, leading to a large pond. He even draws some koi fish in the pond for good measure.

Removing the amount of metal in the façade, he replaces it with sea-worn wooden paneling. Remembering he had met an architect whose specialty was redesigning buildings and common areas for the blind, he knows that different textures have different sounds, which help people who are seeing impaired find their way around. He would incorporate some of those ideas into this building. Ken immediately calls the architect to pick his brain.

After talking to him for an hour-long call, he had some additional ideas to add to his building. He learned that different flooring makes different sounds that blind people can interpret. Lines in the flooring can also help direct them to different areas of the complex. Ken goes about adding these features to his work.

Finishing a rough draft of his building plans, Ken heads over to Morgan's, his junior architect's desk.

"Morgan, I need to redo the designs for Client United Unlimited. Here is my draft. I have built out the design and rough works. I'll start the building plans tomorrow and bring them over for you to add the final changes. We will need them to present on Friday. Doable?"

Taking a quick look at the draft, Morgan smiles. "I love these. Yes, I can get that ready for you by the end of the day tomorrow. These are great." Even Morgan was witnessing the change in Ken. Nevertheless, Ken was oblivious to the changes in his attitude.

The office gossip had already started based on the new spring in his step. Some co-workers had seen smiles cross Ken's face. Everyone suspects a new girl in his life, but none of them had any idea who that would be. Having always been private about his life, his co-workers are only left making their best guesses. And they would only be partly right.

CHAPTER TEN

A nice summer night with a slight breeze adds more enjoyment to tossing the football around. After about an hour and Mykel's friends having to return home, Ken and Mykel take their self-imposed delegated spots on the steps to the house.

Mykel starts in now that he has Ken alone to himself. "So, what do you do?"

"I'm an architect."

"A...art tech?"

"No. An arc-hit- tect. I specialize in designing commercial buildings for large businesses."

"It must be nice to be able to do that. Do you enjoy it?"

"I do," Ken confirms. "I knew it was what I wanted to do when I was young."

"You went to college for it? What is college like?"

Ken isn't sure where the line of questioning is going, but he has a hunch. "I did. Eventually. What do you want to do when you're older?"

"Me? I'll be lucky to be able to go to school." Pausing in his thoughts, Mykel continues. "I might not even be around."

"Do you want to go?" Ken asks, urging an answer.

Mykel's face lit up. "I do. I do."

"Guess what. You can. My family didn't have much money at all. I knew I would have great grades to get into a college, and then I would have to figure out how to pay for it." Ken felt like he was confessing to Mykel more than inspiring him. "I started my college at the cheaper state school level. It was very depressing to me. A major league school is what I wanted. I was acting up because I wasn't where I wanted to be and ended up getting suspended from college."

Mykel couldn't believe what he was hearing. "You what?! Got kicked out of college?"

"You are sworn to secrecy." Ken sticks out his hand to shake the deal. Mykel complies as Ken continues. "Certainly not my best moment. Getting back on track, I excelled in school. I applied for grants and scholarships. I got a few that allowed me to continue my studies at a more prestigious school."

With an expression of bewilderment, Mykel was still looking at Ken's face. It was as if Mykel was studying every feature of Ken's face. Smiling, Ken strikes back. "What?"

"You messed up?"

"Everyone does, Mykel. Everyone does. It is how to handle it that is important." As Ken had bared his soul, he found himself reclining backward on the steps. Truth always comforted Ken, though sometimes he did not want to accept it.

"Wow, there is hope for me yet." Mykel's statement made Ken chuckle.

"What have you messed up?"

"Nothing yet."

"Okay then, answer my question." Ken directs Mykel back to his earlier question.

"Which one? Oh, what I want to do. I think being an art tech. I think that would be cool."

Mykel's mother, Sonya, had been hovering at the screen door. She was enjoying the conversation the two men were having. She always referred to Mykel as her little man. Presently, she was feeling pretty proud of him. Ken was a good influence on him; she decides as she continues to listen in.

"We can start looking at who offers grants for you. There are a lot of organizations that want to help you with your education."

"What is a grant?"

"That's money given to you due to financial need for your schooling, which you don't have to pay back, while a scholarship is based on merit. How are you doing in school? We can look at both."

"You think I can get those?"

"If you want them, Mykel, yes, you can."

"Are you telling me I can go to college?" The mere thought of attending a college brings excitement to Mykel's expression. He had always thought he had no chance of attending any university ever. Now Ken has filled him with hope.

"Mykel, you can do whatever you set your mind to. I am living proof."

Breaking into the conversation, Sonya alerts the two. "Gentlemen, dinner is ready."

"Go wash up, Mykel. I will see you tomorrow."

As Mykel stands, Ken hears a scolding tone from Sonya. "That means you too." Ken turns around to see Sonya staring straight at him. Her gaze was inviting, but her voice was disciplinary in tone. Ken welcomes the offer. It had been some time since he had been at someone else's house for a meal. The invite was uplifting.

Ken happily follows orders, washing up as well, then joining Mykel and his mother at the dinner table; Ken realizes his mouth is already watering. The smell of the fried chicken, cornbread, collard greens, and black-eyed peas filled his nostrils and made him want to dive in. He could tell that prayers were first. He was pleasantly surprised when Sonya added him to her prayer.

"...and we thank you, Lord, for bringing Ken into our life. Keep him. Protect him. Bless him. Amen"

There it was again, a blessing. The allergic reaction to that word wells up in him. He mentally pushes the grief back down. Sonya offers the chicken to Ken and continues to pass along each plate of food to him first. Realizing Sonya was certainly a person who believed in classy traditions, he understood where Mykel had learned to be the same way.

Having been some time since Ken took a meal around a table with a family, he remembers how much he had taken it for granted, scolding his young son, who always wanted to leave the table before he and his wife finished eating. Now he wishes for every moment back —even the frustrating ones.

Breaking the silence, Sonya jumps right in. "I saw you at Cody's funeral. You knew him?"

Ken chokes a little before answering. He appreciates her directness.

"I did, hmm...." Hesitating for a second, he continues. "He tried to rob my house." Ken wasn't sure if he should continue to explain or let it drop. Admitting he had killed his friend James Burns wasn't something he wanted to talk about in front of Mykel. Sonya already knew the story and saved Ken quickly.

"Little man, did I hear you say you want to be an architect too?"

"Mom, it would be great. I could draw buildings all day and get paid." Glancing at each other, Sonya and Ken started laughing.

"Mykel, it is more than that." Ken corrects him. "If fact, if it is okay with your mother, we have a bring your child to work day coming up." Turning to face Sonya, he continues. "If you would allow me to take Mykel to work with me that day, I would be honored." As soon as the words came out, it hit Ken that maybe he should have saved that question for a private discussion.

"Pleeease, Mom. Please. I want to go." Mykel begs.

"Will your homework be done?"

"Yes. Yes."

"Bed made in the morning?"

"Yes. Yes."

Smiling, Ken understood the answer was going to be yes, but Sonya was a very smart woman and was certainly using this request as a bargaining chip.

"If you take the dirty dishes to the sink and head to the bath, I might say yes." Mykel jumps up from the table and gathers all the dishes. Meantime, Sonya invites Ken into the living room to continue talking in private.

"I heard about James and Cody. How does an ordinary architect arm himself quickly and shoot at a person in his house."

"Ordinary?" Ken quips.

"That's what you think was the important part of that question?" she giggles.

"I do." He joins her with a slight chuckle. "Ex-military. I would not have shot at him, but he shot first."

"I don't fault you. I would shoot at anyone entering my house."

"An ordinary mom like you?" Holding up his hand in his defense, he says. "Just kidding." Sonya shoots him a side eye, but she knows she deserves it. She had more questions.

"...but then you came here. Want to tell me why?"

"I had a long conversation with the arresting officer. He told me about Cody and his family. Guess he was already known to the cops. It made me wonder how he got into that situation that night. I wanted to understand more."

Ken sat patiently, knowing even more questions were coming. He understood her wanting to know why he was there and what this all meant to him. If the shoe were on the other foot, he would be doing the same thing.

"You didn't go to the house. Mykel says you were

sitting in your car in front of our house."

"Mykel told you. Your son is amazing. But you know that." Thinking a little bit more about the question, he continues. "I wanted to see where he lives. Then I noticed he might have siblings. I didn't want to be seen there."

"Why?"

"I have, or I should say, had a strong desire to reach out and help him. However, I wasn't sure how to do that. And even more important to me was not being any kind of so-called hero for doing so. I am no one's hero." Dropping his head, Ken feels the pain surging back up in him.

"You have children?"

"Had." Ken did not want to talk about it right then. Sonya's empathy was on high alert as she decided now was not the time to continue down this path of questioning.

"Let me know what date and time you need Mykel to be ready for the day at the office."

"I have a crazy idea…." Ken offers up and goes on to explain his plan for Mykel.

CHAPTER ELEVEN

The clattering of dishes, low-level conversations, and the smell of exquisite cuisine filled the air of the four-star restaurant designed with mahogany walls and leather high-back chairs. Ken was feeling a little pride in himself for being able to arrange a dinner date with Adelle instead of lunch. He planned to be able to spend more time with her than an hour or two—no running back to work for either of them.

Adelle, too, had spoken to her friend Jan, who gave her some great tips on the evening. Adelle loves the assurance Jan gives her on handling topics if they come up or what to do when that 20-minute conversational lull happens. Most importantly, what food not to order when on first dates. This is mainly because it is difficult to eat these foods eloquently. Something that Adelle may not have thought of.

Something was calming about Adelle for Ken. He found himself absorbing it and wanted more. He had made sure to arrive early so he could be seated at the table before her and watch her walk in. Just as the swishing of water filled one of his glasses, he saw her standing at the host podium. Sitting tall in his chair, Ken raises his hand to catch her attention. She returns the gesture with a smile and a small hand wave.

As she headed toward him, he saw her every detail. Most heads in the room did not turn around to see her walk in, but Ken could not take his eyes off her. He has never before seen someone on whom he found himself so transfixed.

"Good evening."

"Hello, Adelle. Glad you could make it," he states as he comes around the table to help her with her chair. Having not been on a date for some time, he didn't know if offering a lady a chair was still acceptable. Adelle did not seem to mind at all. Her expression of joy let Ken relax a little more.

"I have never been to this restaurant. It looks

very nice." Adelle felt the need to start a conversation but knew it was a lame beginning. Luckily for her, lame was where Ken was.

"I do like it a lot. I haven't been here for a couple of years."

"Is there a dish you recommend?" She asks.

"Depends. Meat eater? Fish eater? Or salad eater? You had a salad the other day." He comments.

Blushing as she recognized he had paid attention. It was a nice feeling at the same time. "I do like my salads, but mostly for lunch only." Scrunching her lips together as she thought about what flavors would make her happy tonight, she knew. "Fish."

"Good choice. They have a great Nordic Blue Salmon Almondine and a Chilean Bass. I love both of those dishes."

"Are you having one?" Adelle asks

"I was thinking the sirloin for myself. It has been a while since I have sunk my teeth into actual steak. Hope you don't mind?"

"Why would I mind?"

"People seem easily offended these days if you don't adhere to their beliefs in almost everything, including diet."

"Not me. I can do a good steak too, but tonight it will be the salmon."

Ken loves that Adelle is not easily shaken and speaks her mind freely. If she were offended, he knew she would tell him. She wasn't like other women who might either try to prove their independence and order out of spite or want to prove their femininity by ordering a salad. She did neither.

Adelle was enjoying the fact this meal was truly a date with someone she had noticed a while ago. On her first trip to the office, she remembers passing by Morgan's desk as Ken was spending time with him mentoring his designs. Eavesdropping in on Ken's conversation with his junior architect as she waited to meet the HR specialist, she could tell that Ken was a natural-born teacher with compassion and the desire to help those who wanted to learn. She was drawn in then, but Ken didn't notice her at the moment. His complete focus was on Morgan.

As they enjoy each other's presence, a light conversation continues until their meals arrive. Wine is flowing as the red and white gold flows into their crystal grails. The alcoholic beverage relaxes their thoughts and muscles as well. The food tantalizes their tongues and soaks their breathing. The spirits begin to unleash their inhibitions.

"If you don't mind me asking, how are you doing?" Adelle asks gingerly.

"Doing?" Ken didn't fully comprehend what Adelle was asking.

"Sorry. I am sure it is a touchy subject with you." She continues as Ken recognizes what is coming. "I have heard rumors in your office about the tragedy you have been through."

Taking a hard swallow, Ken was not sure he wanted to ruin the evening with the topic. It certainly was not part of the script he has running in his head on how the night would go. As he chews on his thoughts and sirloin, he weighs his options.

Adelle feels the silence and interrupts it.

"Sorry. Maybe this isn't the time."

"No. Now is fine." Taking in a deep breath, Ken pushes forward. "Just two years ago, my wife, son, and I was heading to the local aquarium. It was midday, and we had just left our house. A drunk young man ran a stop sign at top speed. I never saw him coming. Police estimated he was traveling north of eighty miles per hour." Stopping for a sip of courage, Ken begins to speak again.

Deciding to jump ahead and not speak about the actual scene, "He took my wife and son from me." Tension was building in his chest. Maybe talking about this now was the wrong choice.

"How do you deal with the anger?" Adelle asks in a very compassionate voice.

"Depression. I had depression for some time."

Taking her sip of wine, which was almost a full gulp, she knew better than to question that comment entirely. "No anger?" It was sideways to get to her point.

"Ever have something happen and question why God let it happen?"

"Sure have."

"I can say I still wonder. I still ask."

"As I would too." Adelle offers. Feeling she should share why she was asking such pointed questions, she divulges her grief. "My fiancé was gunned down in a mass shooting several years ago. I asked the same question for a long time. I think I just got weary of it all." She knew it was a big reveal to Ken, but she wasn't done. "One day, I woke up and decided to give my anger back to God. He allowed this; there must be a reason. I know it is a lot easier than it sounds, but something in me was done. I wanted to move on. There has to be more to life than this."

Ken was just listening. He could relate but knows he is not at any point to give up his self-pity just yet. It had been his companion for the last few years. He fears joy, and he knows it.

Adelle elaborates. "Looking back now, I know

my heart's scars and disappointment got me here. These pains taught me lessons from my failures. I guess I learned to appreciate the here and now. Believe me when I say I did not come up with this myself. Someone else did. Someone told me all my experiences, good and bad, have shaped me into who I am today."

Letting her last words hang in the air and rest in her mind, she picks up the dessert menu to offer her a reason to stop speaking and to let Ken just take it all in within his own time.

Placing the dessert menu on the table alerted the server to attend to their table.

"Did you want a dessert to finish the evening?"

Ken's mind snapped to. A restaurant dessert was not his plan for finishing the evening, but it was the perfect tact to change the discussion. "What will the lady have?" Ken offers.

"We will share a crème brulé. Decaf coffee with cream please. No Sugar."

"Great choice. Coffee for me as well. Black."

"Decaf, sir?"

Ken hoped he would have a great reason to burn off any caffeine this late in the day. "Regular, please."

The interruption played well into the conversation. Ken turns the tables on Adelle. "How long have you been running an organization helping people?"

"About five years now. I worked in an office environment like yours when someone came in looking for donations for the poor. My mind could not stop thinking about a friend of mine. She was single, had no children, and needed help. However, few organizations offer up anything for people in that situation. They are very limited. There is a stigma that single people can't ask for help. I wanted to break that."

Ken was astounded at her words. Never reflecting on that issue, he couldn't agree more. Mothers with babies, very low-income families, the homeless, and other politically correct groups got the exposure for help. It made sense to him. However, he was looking to help a woman with a son. Was he doing the same thing?

As if she was reading his mind, she asked another question. "Why are you...." Correcting herself, "What are you looking to do exactly and why?"

"I have met a young man who I think is amazing. He lives with his mom on what others might refer to as the other side of town. I want to be able to offer him opportunities his mom can't afford."

Cutting him off, Adelle was a little confused. "The other day, you said families."

"Yes, families. Him and the other families on his street. Not ready to take on the world." Pausing as he picks his words carefully, "I want to remain anonymous."

"The organization would get credit?"

"I don't care who or what gets credit; I don't want it to be me. I will do whatever it takes to get it done, but I want to be a silent partner."

"Hmm." Adelle sighs.

The crispy crème Brulé was delivered to the table with two spoons. Coffees are set appropriately on each side. Laying the spoons down together in the middle of the table was perfect. Adelle and Ken both reach for the spoons simultaneously and touch. Ken froze for a second before lifting his hand to let Adelle go first. The touch was jolting. Her soft hand reverberated through his body, knowing he wanted more. It was only a second later he realized his dining partner did too.

Adelle scoops a small number of Brulé on her spoon and offers the serving to Ken. With no hesitation, he opens his mouth and takes it in. Using his tongue, he whips the crème from the spoon before releasing it from his lips.

Adelle's plan was moving forward. A little out of her comfort zone, she relished her new ability to make some of the first moves in a relationship. After all, she credits herself with the first move to enter his office. On the other hand, Ken thought he was the mastermind in making reassurances to advance the relationship.

Mimicking her gesture, Ken proceeds to do the same to her. Adelle playfully plays with the spoon with her tongue. Something was swelling in Ken. He knew exactly what that was. It was time to finish the dessert on the table and to make their sweet taste for the evening.

Paying the bill and grabbing their jacket and coat, Ken wraps his arm around Adelle's back as he escorts her to the valet for his car. "You have your car ticket. They can get both cars at once." Ken planned to follow her home, hopefully. But Adelle had plans of her own.

"Oh, sorry. I was dropped off."

Ken's mind screamed inside his head, *Are you kidding me?* "Well then, I can drop you somewhere?"

Mustering up all her strength, Adelle takes her newfound skill and puts it to the test. "Yes. That would be great. How about your place?"

All reasonable thinking had vanished from his mind. As his car pulls up, he immediately opens the passenger door. Adelle steps in and swings her luscious legs to the front position. She ensured her skirt was just a little higher than it had been all evening. Ken knew it would only be a few minutes before his hands roamed all over those legs.

Almost at a run, Ken got to his door. Tipping the guy, he jumps in and looks over at the lovely lady sitting next to him. Ken was beginning to live in the moment. Something he had never really done before in his life. He was known as someone who planned almost everything. Spontaneity had never been a characteristic people would associate with him. If life has taught him anything, it's the fact that life can be short, and planning can be a waste of time. The impulsive feeling gripping him is welcome.

"Make sure your seat belt is on. It might get wild." Adelle just smiles. He had no idea what was coming.

The drive was only a few minutes away from the restaurant. They emerge from his car and enter his house. Before he can close the door fully, Adelle drops her coat and purse on a nearby chair.

As the click of the door lock is the only sound in the room, Ken turns around seeing Adelle standing there. Taking two slow steps, he moves in closer. Adelle does not retreat. She moves in slightly as well.

Uncontrolled, Ken gently pushes Adelle against the opposite wall. Reaching down, he found the soft skin of her lower thigh he had fantasized about all the way home. She let out a quick breath he heard clearly. Pressing his lips to hers, he used the moment to let his hand meander up higher on her thigh. Adelle never trembled. Pushing her body into his, Ken knows the mere act is wanting more.

Still moving his arm upwards, his finger felt the ruffle of her panties. With light pressure on her skin, his finger goes under the fabric and lifts it from her skin. Adelle was excited to jump into the deep end. Her little mental capabilities were clouded with lust, automatically following her desires. Reaching for his crouch, Ken found himself battling his senses. His warmth penetrated her hand.

Not wanting to be restricted to a standing position, Ken takes Adelle's hand and hurriedly leads her to his room. Clothes fly off both bodies as each rips them from the other. Pure sexual pleasure occupied their ambitions.

CHAPTER TWELVE

Monday morning came too soon. Ken spent Sunday bouncing around doing chores at his house while reliving his memories of Friday night. Even though his gardener was due to come by in a day or two, he spent Sunday the old-fashioned way, racking up the fall leaves in his backyard.

It took a couple of days for everything to sink in. Sometimes he felt like his right hand had no idea what his left was doing. The sex was great. What hit him later was the fact they had made love in the bed he shared with his wife. Ken found himself having a hard time reconciling the joy he felt with Adelle and the depression he indulged at the loss of his wife. His inner voice wouldn't let him shake the feeling he just had an affair with his late wife, while logic told him he was being ridiculous.

At least he and Adelle spoke before he drove her home Saturday morning, agreeing not to let his office know of their relationship. At least not yet. Ken did not want to explain anything right now. He prefers to keep his life private. Office gossip wasn't anything Ken participated in, and he already knew he had been the subject matter of a lot of it since the accident occurred. The signs were all there. People shut up as he enters the lunch area for his coffee. He whispered between office staff who thought he could not hear what they were saying. He glances and looks in his direction. Often their assumption was not even close to the actual story. Ken prefers it that way. He did not need their judgment of his lifestyle.

As he entered his office, Morgan was right on his heels.

"Boss. I think you are on to some of your best work. Can you look at these?"

Ken turns to Morgan and gives him his full attention by flipping his lightweight briefcase onto his desk. Morgan flips some large papers across the drafting table. Ken scrutinizes the drawings. Morgan stood patiently waiting to hear Ken's critique of his work. But it did not come.

"These are good. Very good." Ken was pleased. "I see you lengthened the stream a little bit. Good idea. I also love how you have made nooks for small groups of people."

Feeling proud, Morgan ate up Ken's approval of his work. Ken was never demeaning. As a natural teacher, he did praise Morgan often but always provided some additional instruction. Today was the first time Ken did not add to his comments or endorsement of Morgan's work.

"Great. I will prepare it for presentation."

Ken agreed. Morgan snatches up the papers and starts to leave the office. "One more thing Morgan." Morgan's heart sunk. *Here it comes*, he thinks to himself as he stops and turns to face Ken.

Continuing, Ken looks directly at Morgan. "Get a meeting on my calendar. I think it's time to start making you a full architect."

Morgan was speechless. Those words were the farthest thing from his mind. "Yes, sir. Will do." Turning on his heels, Morgan confidently steps out of the office. Ken witnesses the change in his stride and smiles. Morgan had already worked for Ken for just over three years. He was overdue, and Ken knew it.

Adelle's day was also full of Friday night reminiscences. It had been some time for her, and she had never done anything like that.

After returning home Saturday morning, she calls her confidant.

"Jan. It was amazing."

"Hmm, hello to you too. Tell me..." Jan urges.

"He was the perfect gentleman." Adelle starts.

"I hope not too much," Jan jokes.

"Until dessert. I made the first move. You would be so proud of me. I scooped up the pudding on my spoon and then offered it to him. His tongue was amazing." Both ladies giggled. Adelle felt as if she had been transported back to high school.

"He returned the favor, and I went all in."

"You nasty girl." Jan quips.

"We went back to his house. I can say he makes a good breakfast too." Adelle's head was spinning with excitement. Knowing Ken would eventually meet Jan, she keeps several details private.

Adelle was well aware that she would have never made a move on a man in her past life. She had always been shy or played as if she was reluctant as she had always been instructed to do. It was not proper for a woman to let her sexual prowess out. Her newfound empowerment certainly makes her happier on a few different levels, marveling at the times that allow her to be herself instead of pretending to be what she was not.

Knowing she and Ken agreed to keep Friday night their secret, Adelle would have to do her best poker face later that day when she meets up with the executives at his office. Today they were confirming the donation requests for the upcoming winter holidays.

As all the upper management gathered in the

conference room, Adelle kept her head down to avoid eye contact with Ken. Instead of arriving early as he usually did to get his favorite seat, he took a little longer in his office as a stall tactic. Ken could feel the fear in his body that when he saw Adelle for the first time after their encounter, everyone in the room would know about them. Seeing her today could cause a possible issue in keeping their secret quiet. Ken is unsure if he can keep the secret, knowing all he wants to do is take Adelle back home and shut out the world.

Arriving later than usual, Ken is pleasantly surprised to see his normal seat still open. He never realized that every team member had observed his ritual at one time or another, and they all knew that was Ken's seat. He took it right away. He went ahead and did his little ritual of pouring himself some water, but this time immediately began to read the papers in front of his chair.

Nervous to almost shaking, Adelle approaches the front podium to start the meeting. Trying not to look right at Ken, she scans the room quietly. Catching a glimpse of Ken, she notices his head is buried in the pages she had provided everyone. Right then, she knew he had the same plan.

As Adelle spoke to the office team, she relayed what Ken's company had achieved. The company had provided over 50 sleeping bags to donate, 67 used coats, and a financial donation of just over two thousand dollars to Adelle's organization. The number of items and money they were providing overwhelms her. It was late fall, and the winter holiday was just around the corner.

Right then, a commotion was happening right outside the conference window. Several office staff were talking rather noisily. They were in some heavy discussion, loud enough to warrant one of the executives to get up and step outside. Everyone quieted down.

With a very solemn look on his face, the executive returns to the conference room. He leans in and whispers in Ken's ear.

"Someone named Sonya was just rushed to Chicago General."

Ken sits up and turns to face him. "What? When? I have to go." With that, Ken dashes out of the conference room and heads directly for his office. Grabbing his briefcase and cell phone, he races to his car almost at a full run.

Arriving at the emergency room, he looks around at the beds. Mykel spots him first. "Dad. Dad. Over here." Ken heads over to the bed Mykel was next to. Being ignorant of the term Mykel used to call him over; all his energy was driven to finding out what was going on.

Sporting the normal hospital gown, Sonya appears to be exhausted. Mykel wraps his arms around Ken's leg. A bit shocked, Ken certainly did not expect it. "Hey, Mykel. It will be alright." It was instinctive to say those words even though Ken still had no idea what was happening. Ken gently places his hand on the boy's head and gently starts rubbing it.

Pulling the separation curtain from the other side, a male nurse walks in and notices Ken. He is pushing a computer on wheels and has a couple of full

IV bags. "You with Sonya? Can I ask the relation?"

As Ken begins to answer, before he can, Mykel interjects, "He's my dad." Looking down at Mykel in astonishment, he takes a few seconds before he looks back up at the nurse.

"Yep," was all Ken could muster.

Sonya had heard her son's response. At first, she did not know what to make of it, but then she had an idea how that sentence would work in her favor. Just one thing, Ken would have to agree.

All three were pretty quiet as the nurse went about hooking up the IV bag and starting the medicine flow. Taking her blood pressure and oxygen levels, he finishes up this task. Leaving the same way he came in, he pulled the curtain closed behind him.

Leaning in to talk softly, Ken raises the obvious question. "What is going on?"

She chose her words carefully to ensure she did not frighten Mykel. "Seems I have a gallbladder infection. It seems a fall can cause such a thing. Never knew that before now."

"You fell?"

"Yea. I tripped over a loose brick in the backyard and fell. Part of the old firepit went into my side. It was a little bruised. Honestly, I didn't think much about it. I have been clumsy my whole life."

"Has the doctor seen you already?"

"I have to spend the night. Probably a couple of days. They have me on antibiotics." The thought had frightened her a little. She didn't know how to handle Mykel as he couldn't stay at the house alone. "They admit me as soon as they clean up the room assigned to me."

Trying to lighten the topic, Ken tries a little humor. "Room with a window?"

"Hopefully. I did get the discounted price through." Sonya needs to get to the point. "Tomorrow brings your child to work, right?"

"Yes. It is."

"How about you take some of his stuff and bring Mykel to your place for a few days? Can you do that?"

Ken drew the parallel immediately. Mykel had called him dad so Ken could easily leave the hospital with him. Sonya was hoping he could go home with Ken and not to child protective services. Ken would not allow that either. No children should have to be thrown into the system because his mother is ill, and he has no place to go.

"I think that is a wonderful plan. You okay with that, Mykel?"

Shaking his head adamantly up and down, "Yes. Yes." Mykel agrees.

"Okay. Let's wait for your mom to get to her room; then, we will get something to eat. Sound good?"

For the next few minutes, Sonya and Ken play down his mother's condition to let Mykel know she would be fine. In truth, they both knew that might not be the case, but understanding young minds can worry about things adults do not even know they are thinking about, they both wanted to cover their bases with Mykel.

Before they knew it, an orderly appeared and

began getting her ready for her transfer to the new room. Mykel watches every detail the orderly did. He was studying everything that was happening.

"Okay, we are headed to room 103-B. You can follow if you wish."

Mykel leaps up and stands almost at attention.

"Lead on." Ken quips.

"You're her chuf.. er," Mykel struggles to say.

"Chauffeur? You mean Chau-ffeur?" Ken aids Mykel.

"He is her chauffeur." With that, all the adults laugh.

Once in her room, Sonya does her best award-winning scene of being too tired to keep her eyes open. She is fully conscious that Mykel would be persistent and stay until his mom fell asleep. Ken had to suppress his laughter at the whole spectacle.

Convincing Mykel that his mother was fast asleep, Ken coaxes him to leave the hospital for a big fat juicy hamburger and fries at the local drive-in restaurant. Mykel had never been, probably because it was closer to Ken's house than Mykel's.

Ken also knew Adelle had called several times. He had ignored the calls to take care of the situation in front of him. He wanted to get back to her to let her know he was alright and explain what was happening.

CHAPTER THIRTEEN

Waiting in the living room, Ken had some flashbacks of his son getting ready for his first day of preschool. Back then, he sat in the living room waiting for his wife to help finish dressing their son in cute little pants, a shirt, and a vest outfit as if he was a miniature man. The smell of his son's skin fills his emotions.

"No. Geez." came from down the hall.

"Everything okay in there?" Ken yells out.

Ken's plan of getting Mykel a nice work suit and shoes was a great idea. Ken could hardly wait to see Mykel in the outfit. With a look of defeat, Mykel comes from around the corner. He was in a tiny suit jacket, matching pants, a white shirt, and nice shiny shoes which fit perfectly. The tie hung around his neck untied. "I can't get the tie to work."

Mykel's precious expression told Ken it was time to help out. "Come here. Let me show you."

Marching right over, Mykel hands Ken the tie. Getting right to work, Ken went step by step, explaining how to tie it. Within a few minutes, Mykel had become the little man his mother calls him.

"Okay, we need to send a picture of you to your mother."

Mykel smiles, runs over to Ken's briefcase and holds it in his hand. "I'm ready." Snapping a couple of shots, Ken immediately sends them off to Sonya.

Mykel was indeed living up to his mother's nickname of "Little Man." Dressed in his little suit and having the briefcase was so adorable, Ken just wanted to snatch him up and hug him. Knowing Mykel was not his son, Ken held some reservations and held back. Smothering the boy might not be appropriate or may be misread.

The entire drive was filled with Ken talking about his work, daily routines, and whether he or not drinking coffee. Trying not to laugh, Ken addressed every question as professionally as he could.

"Once you get in the office, does your assistant let you know all your calls?" Mykel asks.

"No. I answer my phone. No need for phone messages."

"Does she keep your schedule for you?"

Ken held back his smirk. Mykel's understanding of the workplace was a bit old. "He. And no, he doesn't."

"He?"

"Yes. The person you refer to as an assistant is a 'he.' My computer keeps all my appointments on a schedule now. No need for someone to remind me I have a call or appointment. The computer reminds me."

Mykel's eyes held wonder. "Does he get you your morning coffee?"

"I get my own. Things are very different, Mykel. You will see what I am talking about today."

"I can't wait. I want to be just like you." Mykel blurts out. Ken's astonishment turns to amazement as a sobering flood of emotions swells up in him. Trying to change the topic immediately to avoid Ken's sensations, he shifts the conversation.

"We will visit your mom right after work today. Sound good?"

"Sure does," Mykel replies.

Arriving at Ken's workplace, the little man marches to the front door like a king claiming his new bride. Ken opens the door like Mykel's personal door attendant, standing to the side for Mykel to make his grand entrance. Two female co-workers near the front desk turn to watch Mykel's arrival.

"Oh, he is so cute," quips one.

"He is hired. We need classy men around here." The other one chimes in.

The third one, who is also a part of the welcoming committee, makes the introductions. "And who do we have here?" she inquires.

"I'm Mykel."

Ken quickly corrects him. "Ladies, I want to introduce you to my new junior architect. This is Mr.

Adler."

"Hello, Mr. Adler. I am Ms. Jost. It is a pleasure to make your acquaintance."

The second lady spoke again. "Adler. Like Professor Adler?"

Mykel was a little lost. "I don't know any professors in my family." The ladies giggled quietly since Mykel was answering in a serious tone.

"Well, Mister Adler. If you would come with me. We have a morning presentation on your calendar." Ken observes as Mykel heads off down the hall as if he was the CEO.

"Who is he?"

"A friend of mine. Her son."

"He is so cute."

"Smart and inquisitive too," Ken adds.

Being free that morning, Ken starts making calls regarding the donation project that he and Adelle are working on. He decides to call several of the large companies he has designed buildings for to see if they would be able to donate what he needs. As Adelle had taught him, he had already laid out what he would request from each company. He envisioned these calls being harder to make but quickly found that almost every person he called jumped on board. He was pleased with the results and couldn't wait to tell Adelle.

Before he knew it, lunch had ended, and Mykel bounced back into Ken's office. Anticipating his arrival, Ken had already created a modest work area for Mykel.

"Come over here, Mykel. This is your workstation for today." Mykel heads over and sits in the chair, which is too large for him. He didn't complain. Ken continues as Mykel gets situated. "How did the morning meeting go?" Ken keeps with the theme that Mykel was one of the executives at the firm.

"Wow, you guys do a lot of stuff. Those buildings were amazing."

"Glad you enjoyed yourself. Now I need you to do some work. You good with that?"

"What do you need?"

Ken begins to explain by pointing to a picture on

the top of the desk. "We have been hired to help redesign this building. As you can see, the architecture, or the look of the building, is old. We need to improve the look and feel. Bring it more up to date." Ken looks over at Mykel to see if he understands the direction.

"We start with a pencil drawing. That is your task." Ken reaches over and picks up a basic drawing he had done for another similar building. "As you can see, we don't need great detail. And you can either use the current landscape, bushes, and trees or redesign the landscape. Your choice on what you think looks good,"

Excitement was all over Mykel's face. He studies the picture a little further.

"Do you have any questions for me?"

Mykel had no idea what he should be asking, so Ken hinted. "What kind of business is it? Would that be important?"

"Would it?"

Ken continues to educate Mykel on some of the basic ideas of architecture, explaining how a business could have one look while another might need something completely different and how materials such as wood or stone versus glass and metal give different feels to a building. Not wanting to get too detailed, Ken just gave him some overall direction.

"Think you want to give it a try, Mr. Adler?"

"Yes, sir," Mykel responds. Picking up his pencil, he begins to draw. Ken heads back to his desk. Pretending to dive back into his work, he closely monitors Mykel. The young man was drawing with the enthusiasm of a pro. His eyes were fixed on the page, only periodically looking up at the picture of the old building, and stopping only once in a while to look at his work. Outside of his pencil, the ruler on the desk was getting a workout too.

Mykel was dedicated to his design. Barely even needing to use the eraser, he continues sketching as if he was on a mission. Ken was beginning to wonder what exactly Mykel was illustrating. Walking over, Ken peeks at his work. Mykel had replaced the old appearance of the building with a very modern design. Instead of a solid boring front of the building, it now had a few square corners with elongated windows instead of square ones. The front of the building almost gave the appearance of three buildings with different heights, and the middle building receded just a little. Ken liked the design start. Ken was very impressed.

"This is a very good design, young man. Why did you design the building in squares?"

"You said they made bricks and stone blocks."

"Yes, I did. Very clever."

A clap of thunder roared outside the window. A sudden cloudburst of rain begins to pound the glass. Ken looks at his watch and decides it is time to leave before torrents of rainfall. They had to head over to the hospital to see his mom.

"Let's straighten everything up and head out for the day."

"Can I take this with me?" Mykel asked as he held up his work.

"You most certainly can. Fold it in fours and put it in the briefcase. I am sure your mom will want to see it."

Lightning lit the sky with a pure white streak striking the dark heavens. The rain's intensity was picking up. The roads were still clear, which made Ken glad they left before the normal rush hour traffic would start. Hitting the front windshield, the rain made it appear like silvery liquid sheets while the wipers tapped out their rhythm.

Rain always brought a renewing spirit with it. Ken never shuns the rain. In his younger years, his mother always had to go out and pull him back into the house. The refreshing sense of the rain hitting his skin was like nothing else he knew. Like the fresh snowfall, he would often stand outside with his tongue extended to capture what he could. Never fearing the lightning or thunder, he never had the wisdom to come in. Older now, he understands the possibility of what getting hit by lightning could mean, but he still feels the chances are slim it would ever happen.

"Do you like rain Mykel?" Ken asks.

"Not really. It is loud."

"I have always loved it. Even at a young age my mom would yell at me to come in and I never listened."

"Doesn't the lightning frighten you?"

"Not at all. I do the counting trick."

"What is that?" Mykel asks.

"You can tell what direction the rain is going by counting. Watch." Ken waits for a streak of lightning to light up the sky. "I...2...3...4..." then the thunder hit.

"I don't get it." Mykel says.

"Hold on. Wait for it." The next lightning hit and Ken starts right away. "I...2...3...4...5..." The clap of thunder hits. "Did you notice I got to 5 and almost to 6 this time?"

"Yeah and..."

"That means the storm is moving away from you. Watch next time I will make it to six." The game was making Mykel have more fun than worry. With the next strike Mykel counts with Ken.

"1...2...3...4...5...6..." Thunder roars. Mykel laughs. "That is so cool."

Ken left it at that. He wasn't about to explain that when your count gets shorter it means the storm is coming closer. Ken decides it would be better left for a different day.

Arriving at the hospital, Ken found the closest parking spot he could. He and Mykel were going to have to make a run for it. Dashing to the front doors they both entered, laughing at their race against the elements. Both were wet and were not very successful at staying dry. Ken quickly ran his fingers through Mykel's hair to make it look a little better. Then he does the same to his own. There was only so much he could do at the moment.

Getting to Sonya's room, Ken takes a moment to look over Mykel one more time before letting him enter the room first in his suit and tie carrying his briefcase. Ken could hear Sonya the moment Mykel enters. She had known that Ken had bought the suit as he told her the night at dinner what he wanted to do for "bring your child to work" day. She had only wished she could have been at home with him as he dressed.

"Well look at you my little man."

"Hi mom."

"You look sharp. How was your day at the office?" She asks as Ken enters the room and leans against the door.

"We were busy all day. They put me to work. Let me show you." Reaching for the briefcase, he begins to pull out his drawing. Sonya snuck a glance over at Ken to acknowledge her appreciation of all he had done for her son.

"Look mom," Mykel says as he proudly holds up his work.

CHAPTER FOURTEEN

The rain pelts the roof with such force that it sounds like it's trying to find a way in. Checking her windows to see if there were any leaks, Adelle walks around the entire house. She knows that soon the rain will give way to snow, making driving a little more difficult. Therefore, she never let the rain bother her. It was the lesser of two evils in her mind.

Working remotely for her organization has its advantages. Today is one of those days. After checking all the potential areas of the house that could leak, satisfied everything is good; she goes back to work organizing her files on the different charity events she has going on. It is second nature to her.

Thinking about the other night with Ken, she isn't sure if she should be a bit embarrassed at her advances or revel. She built up her confidence to make the moves. She remembers that Jan told her how proud she was that she was feeling more empowered and that it appears Ken enjoys it as much as she does. Smiling to herself as the evening replayed in her mind, she knew one thing, she enjoyed herself.

Rainy days like these brought her back to the age of nineteen. She is old enough to move out of her parent's house but too afraid to do so. The world back then was a very scary place to her. Her parents did not shelter her, but they did not push her either. They were happy that their daughter was a good daughter who did not cause them any concerns.

Her mother did not have to work since her father brought good money. Spending her time doing church charity work, Adelle would go with her to help whenever she could. There was one thing Adelle saw a bit differently, though: the people the church would help versus those they did not. Being a single woman with no children, she noticed little to no charities they could turn to for help. A good number of women living in their cars bothered her. There were numerous charities for families with children, pregnant women, and people with disabilities.

Wanting to help a few women she had come across, who parked together for safety reasons, she began to deliver simple items like toothbrushes, wash wipes, and food. These simple acts led her to start her organization that raised charity funds where she found the needs were not as conventional as other charities.

She never realized how much it takes to run a charity. Getting the funding is a lot of work, and it takes a lot of courage to ask for the funding. She had to learn that being shy would not get it done.

Extreme hot, rainy, and snowy days were reminders that not everyone has a roof over their head. Though more shelters opened in the winter, there was never enough or a way to get them to the locations other than on foot. One day she had the idea for a charity that would be able to get volunteers to drive vans around the city and pick up anyone who wanted a ride to a shelter. That became her second charity.

Before she knew it, she was running four different charities. And now she felt as if she and Ken were starting the fifth one. Project Celebrate a Street is in the throes of something new. Working with Ken made this project even more rewarding than overseeing others alone.

Being in and out of Ken's office over the past couple of years let her hear all the office gossip. She only came on the scene after Ken had lost his family. The office staff often spoke about his pain and how he had become quieter over the years. Adelle knew making advances back then would not be appropriate or probably welcomed. She also knew he had to find his way through his sorrow.

Never being the type of woman who felt she should try to fix someone. She prefers helping someone instead. She didn't know Ken well enough to offer anything. Her charities had nothing to do with the tragedy he was experiencing.

As the rain escalates, the roar sounds like she is in the middle of a functioning machine. Periodically the room would light up from the flashes of lightning followed by the boom and crackle of thunder. The light show stops her for a second as she looks outside the window to see the show mother nature is performing.

Studying Ken over the past couple of years, Adelle acted on instinct. She knew she had seen a slight turn in his attitude. He was smiling a little more. His appearance was fresher and a tiny bit cleaner. He had never let his looks deteriorate, but the bags under his eyes disappeared. There was just something new about him that Adelle had noticed.

Debating for a few weeks before approaching his office, Adelle was driving herself nuts. *Should I? Maybe he will reject me? Maybe he is not ready, and I am jumping the gun.* Everything Adelle's mind could come up with sounded corny to her. She started running her thoughts by Jan, who supported a couple of her ideas.

That particular day she walked to his office door. She had woken up determined. She stopped her mind from coming up with any negative thoughts. When one bad thought came to the forefront of her mind, she pushed it right back out. She treated the thoughts about Ken as if she were asking someone for funding. She dwelled more on the future than the past, hoping she was making a wonderful change.

Without notice, the sky lit up, thunder crashed, and the power went out. Adelle instinctively knew at the first sign to hit the save button just before things went black. She sits down in her chair and stares up at the window again. The rain is coming down in sheets now, giving a translucent look to everything outside.

Her cell phone rang. Looking at the screen, she knew it was Russell. He was one of the volunteer van drivers, probably checking in.

"Hello."

"Hey, Adelle. Just checking in. We have driven all over the city and brought in about twelve people who needed a ride to the shelter. We don't see anyone else who wants to go in. Think we are good today."

"Thanks, Russell. Appreciate the update. Rain is getting worse, and we just lost power."

"Everything okay with you?"

"Yea. I'm safe."

"I will drive back to the shelter and see if they have power." Russell quips.

"Thanks. We have a generator if they need one." Adelle was pleased to know that they were able to help some people. She also appreciated Russell, one of the volunteers who always went above and beyond what was necessary. She felt very fortunate to have him on her staff.

Not knowing how long the power would be out, Adelle decides to move over to her high-backed chair and take in the sounds of the rain after getting herself some hot Earl Grey tea. The tea is comforting to her. The blackout to her was a godly message that she should take a break.

She couldn't remember the last time the rain had come down so hard, but she didn't mind it. Showers bring life and renewal with them, even though they could spell disaster in other places. Since her house wasn't near any rivers, mountains, or other potential overflows or landslides, the rain was never really a concern to her.

Closing her eyes, she concentrates on the sounds. Mother nature is a wild beast at times. It brought her the idea that women hold those same qualities. Phrases like "don't get between a momma bear and her cub" are often used to represent mothers protecting their children. Her mind wanders to mother nature's strength, and she hopes that one day she can see herself as strong.

She decides at once to stop doubting her moves with Ken. After all, he did not seem to disagree with her suggestions, verbal or otherwise. He has never treated her with any degrading notions as some men had in the past. So many assumptions are still held by many who think an assertive woman is an easy mark or promiscuous.

With Ken, the feeling felt mutual. He treated her as an equal and appeared to enjoy not having to always be the one to make the first move. She grins as she remembers a couple of his first moves. She had no objections to those either.

CHAPTER FIFTEEN

Mykel crawls into his mother's hospital bed to snuggle with her while he tells of the day's events. He beams with pride as he speaks to her about the morning meeting, followed by the building he designed. Soon his words start to trail off as his eyes slowly close. Eventually, he was fast asleep in his mother's arms.

"Thank you," Sonya whispers to Ken.

"It was my pleasure." Ken decides he should move his chair closer so they can talk without raising their voices, allowing the little man to sleep.

"I know you gave money to Cody's family for the headstone. That was nice of you. But you know it wasn't your fault? You had nothing to do with his death."

"The money wasn't a guilt thing. The preacher had told me that she had another child buried there too.

He also said there was no headstone for either child. That just isn't right. I knew I could do something about that." Ken admits.

"You have a good heart." Sonya wants to point out that fact because she felt Ken was unaware.

She was right. Ken was shaking his head no. Though others have made the same suggestion, Ken tends to tell himself he could do more than he did. Even with the accident. Maybe he could have seen the oncoming car and prevented the accident. Having not spoken about his broken heart out loud, he was about to. "My heart hurts. I don't know that is a good thing."

Sonya's motherly instinct kicks in even though Ken is her age. She could see the pain. "Broken hearts can be mended." She proclaims. "They can heal without you giving up your memories. Our hearts can teach us what is truly important to us: life.

"I miss them greatly." Choking his comments, Ken could barely get the next few words out. "I failed them."

The last words hung in the air for a few seconds

before crashing into Sonya's heart. "You are talking about your child? You mentioned it before. Do you want to talk about it?"

Sitting in silence for a little while longer, Ken agrees to talk. After all, he had recently just told Adelle about it. He was finding that the second time wasn't any easier. "It was a perfect day. We were all heading out on what we always referred to as an adventure. My son loved the ocean. He could not get enough of being on the lake. He always said he wanted to be an ocean diver." Taking a deep breath, he pauses to get the lump in his throat to pass. Sonya remains quiet, awaiting his next remarks. She knows he is searching for words he can speak. Sonya sees some tears forming in his eyes.

"Mel and I wanted to take Clint to the local aquarium. We had a very special surprise for him. We had arranged for him to be able to feed the fish in the large tank. It was a kid's event." Ken breaks off. He can no longer hold his tears back. Ken strangled the cry of frustration. Reaching for the tissues on the table next to Sonya's bed, he blew his nose. Reaching for a second tissue, Ken felt the instability in his body, knowing he had a great need to vocalize his torment. He begins fighting the desire to release it all, sucking his feeling back in. The hard swallow helps this time. Ken knows that one day soon, nothing will stop the flow of his emotions. Now was not the time.

"I was a bit irritated at the fact we were running a little late." This was the first time Ken had admitted this point to anyone. Ken felt a little relief knowing it was out in the open. "I am not sure how clearly, I checked for oncoming traffic, but it was a four-way stop. The guy came crashing through the intersection, hitting our car. He was speeding. Before I knew what was happening, our car spun around like a top. My wife's long hair was caught in the rearview mirror. Her side of the car was smashed in at least a foot. My son was sitting behind her."

Sonya let out a sigh. She could not imagine what it must have been like. She notices that her sound has brought Ken's words to a halt. Trying to reassure him, she mutters, "How could you have known?"

Continuing to speak without acknowledging her

words, Ken describes some of the aftermaths. "My son was thrown around the back of the car. His blood was everywhere. My wife made some sounds, but it was apparent her head hit the side window first during the crash, bashing in her skull before her hair got tangled."

Knowing those images would never leave him, Sonya sat silently with him. He dabs his eyes in a hopeless attempt to keep his cheeks dry. His eyes swell, turning red. The fatigue comes over Ken, but he knows he must get it together to get Mykel back to his house. He could not afford to explore his emotions now.

Excusing himself from her bedside, he goes into her washroom to freshen up and pull himself together. He is unsure if he could. Ken shields his face from the mirror so that he would not see the appearance of his eyes and emotions. Splashing water on his face a couple of times in hopes of cooling off his emotions, he grabs a towel and shoves his face into it. If he were at home right now, he probably would have yelled into the towel, but he did not have that option.

Trying a quick breathing exercise, Ken takes in a

deep breath and starts to mentally count to ten. Then he let the breath out, gradually counting to ten again. He does this trick a couple more times until it gets easier. Concentrating on the counting and breathing brought him back from his reminiscence.

Affording himself a glance in the mirror, Ken checks to see if his feelings are still obvious. His eyes were still slightly red, but allergies could be the excuse. Coming back out of the bathroom, he walks over to Sonya.

He wants to leave and discontinue the conversation. Sonya was at a loss for the right words but felt compelled to say something. "I am so sorry." Everyone was sorry. Ken knew that. There was nothing anyone could do about it.

"Thanks," was his automated response. "I think Mykel needs to get to bed."

Sonya agrees. Walking over to the other side of the bed, Ken softly puts his arms under Mykel. Lifting him off his mother, Mykel barely stirs. Sonya reaches out and touches Ken's arm as if to say, *"I wish I could fix this for you."* Ken locks eyes with her for a split second. He couldn't hold the stare any longer without bursting out again.

Taking Mykel home keeps Ken from going back over the evening's conversation. Once home, Ken carries Mykel into Clint's old room. Undressing him and putting the young man in his pajamas, something Ken had done a hundred times before with his son, he tucks him into bed.

Standing back, he looks down at the boy in his son's bed. His posture begins to collapse. He can no longer hold his weight. His knees buckle underneath him, forcing Ken to sit on the edge of the bed. The tears he held back earlier now overpower him. With his head in his hands, the tears begin to flow. He didn't want to wake up Mykel and attempted to be silent. However, he suddenly felt a tiny hand on his back. Turning around to look, Mykel was sitting up.

In a young voice, he spoke, "I wasn't asleep at the hospital. I heard it all." Reaching for Ken's hand, Mykel gently pulls Ken to his side as he moves over to the bed to give Ken room. At the invite, Ken lies down next to Mykel. Slowing his breathing, Ken settles down. Closing his eyes, Ken felt like his Clint was lying next to him again. The fantasy felt good. Soon they were both asleep.

CHAPTER SIXTEEN

With everything rinsed by the rain, puddles remain in the low-level grass and street curbs that attempt to hold onto the precious moisture. The birds had come back out and graciously offered their voices of the song. The hope that came with the rain was also on Ken and Mykel's minds when doctors released his mother from the hospital in good health.

Those few days Mykel had stayed with Ken brought its renewal of heart. Ken continues to ache over Clint's death. However, the house felt alive for those few short days. The rekindled silence that was present again before Mykel moved in was back. This time the quietness was unwelcome. He was thirsting for something more.

Ken fights the invasion of a soundless night as he decides to let the bedroom fans make a white noise background. He knows he must get some sleep tonight. He is presenting his latest designs to the client in the morning and meeting with Adelle again. Business was business, but his latest work is certainly a reflection of his new position in life. Going to bed a little earlier than normal, Ken fell asleep quickly. Morning came just as fast.

He was proud of his work and hoped the client would be too. Almost every staff member in the office that has seen his latest drawing was impressed with the design.

Before he knew it, Ken found himself completing his presentation with Morgan at his side. Morgan had created a 3D image of the design to help seal the deal with the client, adding some live-looking waterfalls into the plans.

"Integrating the surrounding landscape, adding some areas within the complex to bring the beauty of nature, gives your employees reason to go outside and soak in some real sunlight."

Pausing for effect, Ken continues as the 3D 360

design whirls around slowly, showing the clients every angle and aspect of the complex exterior. "As we circle back around, imagine yourself holding a meeting in the outdoor arena, which doubles as a great place to lunch near the pond when not being used by employees."

After completing his presentation, he sits back down, awaiting the clients to evaluate his work. But instead, Ken hears clapping. Looking back, he realizes that the clients are standing and applauding the proposal. He was a bit stunned. Having received compliments in the past, applause is something new.

"Thanks. I appreciate it."

"This is more than what we ever thought we would get back. You have ideas that never crossed our minds here, but we now know we need." One of the clients offers up.

"Great. We have a deal then?"

"Yes. Next steps."

"We will have something for you in the next ten days. Sound good?" The clients agree and head out of the office. As a reward for such great work, Ken hands over the project to Morgan. It is a win-win for both to feel Morgan is raring to go and freeing up some time for Ken to continue to work on the charity project.

Ken's heart rose in anticipation of seeing Adelle shortly. Deep down, Ken knew it was probably wishful thinking that Adelle wanted what he wanted. He fears he might be moving too fast. Turning up the ringer on his phone out of precaution in case Adelle called and canceled the evening. Ken found himself thinking he did not have a right to be happy. He could devise reasons why Adelle might call it off even though she never even hinted that she would do that.

Meeting Adelle and being with her is against everything Ken knew to be him since the last of his wife. Against everything he was taught about how he should act with a lady. Against the story, he had been telling himself how his life would go. Adelle and Mykel came out of nowhere. But his heart maintains a willingness to take all the risks.

Needing permission from the most important people in his life, Ken decides to make one stop on his way to her house. Pulling into the cemetery, driving directly over to his wife and son's graves, he parks. Setting to the headstones, Ken crouches down and begins talking to his family.

"I miss you so much. I am sorry I have not come around as much as I should. It rips me apart every time I think about that day. I become unhinged." Ken starts to quiver. In an apologetic tone, "I should have seen that idiot was driving too fast. You know I was frustrated that we left late. I let my emotions make my decisions. Please forgive me." Lowering his head as if in prayer, Ken sucks in the air around him as his cheeks swell and releases the air back out as he contemplates his next words.

Through a crackling voice, Ken pushes out his next words. "You know you are my true love. I also know you would never want me to suffer for the rest of my life, though I sometimes feel I deserve it." Hesitating for a second, he decides to force himself to keep speaking. "I have met someone, Mel. She is a nice lady who cares much about others, just like you." Still staring at the grave, Ken half expects something, expecting punishment. Nothing came.

Lifting his eyes to glance at Melissa's name on her headstone, Ken felt electricity go through him. More of excitement or approval than it was retribution. Strength begins to fill his body, but his affirmation is not over. "I will not forget either of you. You are my life today as you were when we married. Clint has been my son always. You cannot be replaced." Pausing for a moment. "Ever."

Still crouched down, Ken sits in silence and listens to the wind lightly blowing in the trees. Two blue jays flew down, landing on the top of Melissa's tombstone. Not one muscle moved in Ken's body. He was sure Melissa and Clint were sending him a message of approval. After a few moments, both birds flew off.

Reaching his hand to his lips, he kisses his hand and then places his hand on the headstone. He repeats the action with Clint's headstone. Rising from the grave, Ken stands there for another few seconds.

"I love you both. Thank you." Starring at the place they now rest, Ken starts to feel the flaw in his plan. Maybe coming here before visiting Adelle was not the best idea. Melissa weighed on his heart, but he felt the message was clear for him to continue finding his happiness. Gathering himself, he heads back to go to his destination.

Ken pulls up to Adelle's 1914 house in Chicago Heights. The two-story house has a grand entrance with stairs bordered by a white railing, leading to a porch that goes all the way across. The overhang also goes across the porch area, with a nice living room window to the left of the large wooden door. The house has light yellow brick halfway up the wall and yellow wooden blanks to the roof.

Two windows peer out into the street from the second story. The house trim is a bright white, and overall is cozy, quaint style home. A couple of nice large hanging ferns make the home even more welcoming. The house fits Adelle's personality to a "T."

Parking out front, Ken heads to her front door, but it swings open before he can knock on the door. Adelle was just heading out to her car with a box of donations to throw into her trunk.

"Hello."

"Hi. Sorry, I wanted these items out of the way before you got here." Adelle confesses.

"Let me help. Where are you taking them?" Ken offers.

"To put them in my car. I have to take them to a shelter in the morning." Pulling out her keys, she clicks on the remote and lets the trunk pop open. "If you could just slide them to the right. That would be great." The trunk was already full of a couple of other boxes and bags. The only open area was to the right.

"Looks like you have some goodies for some people."

"People have been very generous."

As they stroll back to the house, Ken gets a bit curious. "Do you do all your deliveries too?"

"No. No. But there are some places I do like to visit, and I hate to go empty-handed."

Stepping back into the house, Ken lets Adelle

enter first, being the perfect gentleman his dad had taught him to be. Ken has never held the thought to be otherwise, regardless of modern-day beliefs.

"I have everything set up over here." Adelle points to the large table in her dining area.

Heading over to the table, Ken takes in the house's architecture. "When was this house built? 1913? 14?"

A little stunned, Adelle replies. "1914. You know your field of work."

Being a little mischievous now, Ken decides not to explain that his parents owned a similar house built in 1913; he would just let her think he knows everything about his field.

"Anything to drink? I have a nice raspberry iced tea."

"That sounds refreshing." As Adelle disappears into the kitchen, Ken glances around the house to see what is where. He guesses the bedrooms are all upstairs and expect to find out a little later in the evening.

Popping back in, Adelle hands him his drink and a coaster. "Okay, this is what I have so far." Adelle gets right to the point. She begins to check off each item of their plan as if she were finishing a long to-do list. With only a few more weeks to pull off this scheme, Ken was happy to see that most of the pieces were already in place. Wondering if Adelle was always this focused when going through a project, he had stopped hearing her words and was staring at her.

Adelle knew it as she looked up and caught his eyes. "Are you still with me?"

Her tone fractures the notions bouncing around in his head as Ken realizes he has been caught. "Yes. I am with you." His thoughts complete the sentence in his head "*and want to be wiiitthh you.*" The idea illuminates Ken's face before he can stop it. His expression says it all.

As if reading his mind, Adelle responds, "Sooner we cover this information, the sooner we can uncover other information," she says with a cheekiness. "Have some iced tea. Cool down, cowboy."

Transparency was never a strong trait in Ken.

Keeping most things private, he has a habit of keeping people at arm's length in most relationships. This shift is obvious to him. As far as he is concerned, everyone can see right through him. Sooner than later, the whole office will know what is up. Normally, that would be a concern for him, but having gone through as much as he has over the last few years, he no longer cares. He no longer wastes his energy, hiding how he is feeling and what he is doing. He no longer cares who knows what.

"I apologize. The way you organize all these tasks is astonishing."

"That is the Virgo in me. Organization."

Smiling, Ken adds to that list. "I always heard that Virgos are very helpful. Always the ones to help first."

"That could be my problem." Adelle giggles. "So, did you hear anything I said?"

"I did. What is left to do?"

"Easy, but time-consuming things. We need to call each person or company that committed to participate in making sure they are on track and have the right information."

"I can do that." Ken offers.

"We both can. Divide and conquer." With that, Adelle offers up some dinner. "I thought I would cook some tuna cakes for dinner. Are you okay with tuna?"

Ken had forgotten it was dinner time. He had so much on his mind he neglected the fact he had not eaten a lot today. "That sounds great. Can I help?"

Adelle shoots him a look that Ken catches. "What?"

"Oh, I am putting you to work. I even have an apron for you. Come on. Get to work." Adelle declares as she enters the kitchen. Being obedient, Ken follows. He notices that she has already prepared the ingredients on her kitchen island. She hands him an apron that is anything but manly, bright pink and white, with ruffles on the bottom of the apron skirt. Ken chuckles.

Watching Ken's expression, Adelle adds to his expression. "I hear real men wear pink."

Feeling feisty, Ken's quick comeback throws

Adelle off her game for a second. "Yes. I could just wear the pink apron." Leaving her speechless as the image of him almost naked in just the apron runs through Adelle's mind, she blushes a little.

"Maybe later. I am hungry, and we will never get a meal on the table if I do that."

"That's for sure. Can you please cut the chives for me?" Adelle pleads.

Adelle's apron was designed like a fancy nineteen-fifties dress in a soft blue, with plaid bows on the top and each pocket, with the same plaid as a bottom ruffle. She starts adding the ingredients to a bowl. First, the drained tuna, eggs, salt, pepper, and his cut chives. She hands him some parsley to chop as well. She blends the ingredients, makes several patties, and cooks them in the pan.

"I have some nice white wine behind you if you would do the honors." Adelle invites. Ken washes his hands and goes over to pick a nice bottle of wine. Grabbing the wine opener, he pops the bottle. She had already set the kitchen bar that faces the outside backyard window. It was a great view.

Ken pours the wine into the glasses as Adelle brings the meal over. "Dinner is served." The dinner salad was already on the table, along with the dressing and dill sauce for the tuna cakes. Everything looked scrumptious and smelled delicious.

The meal ends up being secondary to the conversation as they continuously speak about dreams, a little bit about their personal histories, and funny things they have each experienced in their lifetimes so far. As they enjoy the discussion, the cuisine just seems to disappear.

"You mentioned that you have always wanted to travel. Where would you go first?" Ken asks Adelle.

"I think Greece or France. Both sound romantic. How about you?"

Ken had not truly considered traveling aboard. He was perfectly content jumping in a car and hitting a nice hotel with room service. That made him happy. His younger years included some camping. He did take his son a couple of times, but he still preferred the comfort of plush rooms.

Answering her question, Ken feels a little understated. "I would love to take a train to California and venture up or down the coast. I would love to spend more time in the Pacific Ocean." Adelle tilts her head as if that were a good idea.

They pick up the dishes and move them to the sink without missing a beat. Adelle refills the wine glasses as she heads to the living room. Ken follows. Sitting in the middle of the couch, Ken could sit right next to her or in another chair. Deciding to take on her challenge, he scoots right next to her.

With the lingering effects of having a full belly, Ken fights an overwhelming feeling of wanting to nap. Though he knows his next words are a bit lame, he says them anyways as the silence becomes awkward. "That was a tasty dinner. Everything was perfect."

"We can make it a bit more perfect," Adelle suggests.

"And how would we do that?" Ken asks, knowing exactly what Adelle has hinted at. Leaning in, he kisses her. Adelle knows she wants more. They both contributed their dessert when the night was about to get hot.

CHAPTER SEVENTEEN

Ken could feel his cell phone vibrating. Deciding not to answer it, he and Adelle continue to talk. He was enjoying the conversation. Then he felt it vibrate again. Ken ignores it one more time. But another call came in before he could pull it out to turn it off. Pulling the phone from his pocket, he notices Sonya Adler is calling.

"I need to answer this, sorry," Ken says to Adelle as he answers his cell phone. "Hello."

Adelle could hear her through the phone. "Hurry. I need you to come over. Mykel has been arrested."

"For what?"

"Burglary."

"Burglary. What?" Ken was confused. He never thought Mykel would commit a crime like that. "We are on our way."

Getting dressed quickly, they both rush around for a few minutes. Adelle grabs her purse. Ken reaches for his keys as they jointly run out to his car. Driving faster than normal, Ken could not get to the Adler's fast enough. As they pull up, he sees Mykel in the back seat of a squad car. Mykel's expression says it all. He is frightened to death. Jumping out of his car, Ken runs over to the nearest officer.

"What is going on here? Why do you have Mykel in the car?"

"Calm down, sir. Calm down." The officer repeated. His suggestion only annoys Ken more.

"Tell me right now what is going on," Ken demands.

"A witness has named Mykel in a recent robbery of a convenience store. We should check out every lead."

"Checking out a lead is one thing. You have him under arrest sitting in your car."

"We want to take him to the station to interview. He is not under arrest at this time."

"Not without an adult. And a lawyer." Ken challenges the officer.

"What store? When?" Sonya asks between tears.

"We will discuss the charges at the station."

Sonya breaks away from the officer keeping her from Mykel and runs to Ken's side.

"Help us. My baby didn't do this." Ken puts his arm around her and holds her.

"We will go to the station with Mykel and sort this out. Do you have an attorney?" The officer asks.

Sonya shakes her head no. "I know some." Ken turns to look at the officer. "What station are you taking Mykel to?"

"The Larabee Station."

"Fine. We will follow you. Do not interview him without one of us present." Turning to Sonya, he continues. "Close up the house and come with us."

Adelle had been right at Ken's side during the whole ordeal. She knows he will want to call his attorney on the way over to the station, so she makes

Ken an offer.

"Want me to drive?"

"You know the way there?"

"Sure do. I work with several stations in the area as donors to my causes."

"Great." Without thinking, Ken grabs Adelle's hand as he walks with her back to the car. Opening the driver's side car door, she slides in. His actions are not lost on her. She can't remember the last time a guy opened a car door for her like this, and he has performed this loving action twice in the last hour. She knows Ken's behavior is natural, and she appreciates it.

Giving her some directions as they wait for Sonya to lock up and slide into the back seat; once they're heading directly to the police station, Ken starts making some calls.

"Steve, hi, it's Ken." Pausing for a moment to listen to Steve on the other side of the call, he continues. "I need your help. We are heading to the Larabee Station, where a young man I know has been brought in under the robbery charge. I know him and don't believe it to be true." Pausing again before continuing. "Yes, if you could. His name is Mykel Alder. I appreciate this."

Clicking the phone off, Ken turns to Adelle and Sonya. "My friend Steve is going to meet us there. I am sure we will get there first. He said to not let Mykel answer anything until he gets there."

"Understood." Glancing worriedly toward Ken, Sonya was at a loss. She has never been in this position but has heard many horror stories from others. The fear of her son going to prison for something she knew he would never do overwhelmed her. She was thinking the worst.

Adelle and Ken could hear Sonya as she began to cry softly. Being in the front seat, Ken could not comfort her the way he normally would.

"I'm sorry this is happening. Steve is the best. We will get this all figured out."

Chiming in, Adelle speaks up. "Knowing Ken, he will do everything he can to help." Sonya finds the words comforting. Snapping up a tissue, she dots her eyes and takes a deep breath.

"Thank you." Hesitating a bit, she continues, "I don't know what I would do without you."

The remaining drive to the station was silent, except for Sonya's sniffles.

Arriving at the modern-day police station with fancy glass window panels and a fresh design, it looks more like an office building than a law enforcement structure. That did not change Ken's attitude about the pending arrest and what he was now considered a young man being stereotyped.

Heading to the front desk, Ken did not wait to be asked anything. "We are here for Mykel Alder. He was brought in a few minutes ago. This is his mother."

The front desk officer takes a moment to look at the logbook and sees Mykel's name. "Investigation room 3. I will let the officer and detectives know you are here." She steps away from the desk and returns shortly. "He will be right out."

Starting to pace, Ken is getting antsy. The mere thought of Mykel being alone in the police station and knowing he is being accused of something he did not do, was pulling at his heart. Before he could fully imagine the panic Mykel was going through, Ken heard, "Right this way, folks."

Following the detective into the back area, Ken was disappointed to hear that Mykel was already in an interrogation room. "Can we see him?"

"Not right now." The detective instructs.

Every word was aggravating Ken. Everything he has seen and heard so far was not boosting confidence levels. "Is he alone in there? Can you tell him his mother is here?" The detective nods, agreeing to let Mykel know that information.

"You can step in here to view him in the room. No touching or tapping on the glass. Just observe." The detective opens the door next to the interrogation room. Stepping in, the three peer into the cold, harsh room where Mykel was sitting alone. His eyes were as wide as can be. Unable to sit still, his mom reaches to touch the glass as if to transport herself into the other room.

"No touching the glass." The detective reminds

everyone.

"Tap, tap, tap" was heard on the viewing room door. The detective opens the door to see Steve standing in the doorway. Immediately put out his hand to introduce himself. "Hello, I am Steve Nichols. Mykel Alder's attorney."

"Detective Jack Thompson. Shall we go in?" Motioning the direction and opening the door, Steve follows the detective into the cold gray room.

"Hi, Mykel. Your mother hired me to represent you. How are you doing? Are they treating you well?" Mykel signals that he is okay. "I want to sit next to you. Can you move over a tiny bit?" Snatching a metal chair against the wall, Steve moves it next to Mykel on the same side of the table and sits down. Pulling out a legal pad from his briefcase, snapping his pen open, he gives Mykel one more glance before acknowledging the detective to begin.

"Please state your full name for the record." The detective directs Mykel.

"Mykel John Adler."

"M-I-C-H..."

"No. M-Y-K-E-L."

"Thank you. J-O-H-N and A-D-L-E-R, correct?" the detective asks.

"Yes, sir."

"You have already been read your rights. Do you understand them?"

Steve glances over at Mykel. "Is there anything you have questions about?"

Holding back tears, the little man shakes his head no. Steve looks back at the detective, "We can continue."

Ken's annoyance was increasing. He strongly feels there is no reason that Mykel should be going through this questioning and embarrassment. His anxiety is making him begin to pace while not taking his eyes off Mykel. If it were his son, he had no idea how we could remain on this side of the glass. Ken was fighting the urge to bust into the interrogation room and grab Mykel to take him home. But he knows better than even trying.

Adelle does not know how she can help Ken settle down. At this very moment, she had her arm around Sonya in an attempt to console her. Her goal was to lend her strength to Sonya so she could focus on her son. After all, Ken was a grown man, and Mykel was truly the person here who needed everyone's full attention.

Being direct, the detective asked the main question. "Did you participate in the robbery or have any knowledge of the robbery at the Stop Quik convenience store last Wednesday late afternoon?"

"No, I did not." Mykel blurts out.

"An eyewitness has come forward that has stated you were there. How do you explain that?"

"They are wrong."

"Where were you that day?"

"I don't know." Mykel quickly replies. Steve put his right hand on Mykel's left shoulder.

"Before you continue, try to think back."

Ken's anger was reaching an all-time high at this point. He could see the panic in Mykel and knew there was no way Mykel could think under this stress. Right then, Adelle comes over and touches Ken's back. He was in no mood to be reassured right now.

The detective went over the questions even though Mykel answered them all. "Why would someone say you were part of the robbery Mykel?"

"I don't know." Mykel begins to cry.

"This has been asked and answered. Move on." Steve instructs the detective.

Spurring Mykel on, the detective continues. "I'm guessing when we get the video from the store, you will be on it."

Shaking his head, no, Mykel has stopped talking. He is frustrated because no one is listening to him.

"That's enough for today," Steve says. "Are we free to go?"

Looking over at Steve, he could see the disgust on his face. "Fine. Don't leave town. We should have the videotape tomorrow. We will probably be back to arrest you then."

Knowing the last words the detective spit out were unnecessary, Steve claps back, "Enough. Until you have solid proof, you will not contact my client." Standing up to leave, he reaches out with his card. "Here is my card." Turning to Mykel and directing him to the door, "Let's go."

Walking out to the hallway, Mykel is devoured by his mother, who fears she will not see him for some time. She pulls him close.

Ken thanks Steve for everything he is doing for them. "Thank you for coming out here. I owe you one."

"I didn't do anything. Anytime you need me, just let me know." Steve shakes hands with Ken as they all head out of the building. "If Mykel wasn't there, then the video from the store should exonerate him," Steve adds.

"I agree. But this detective seems to have his heart set on charging Mykel." Ken admits.

"Not to worry. I have his back." Slapping Ken on his back gently, Steve parted ways with the group as Ken, Adelle, Sonya, and Mykel headed for Ken's car to return home.

CHAPTER EIGHTEEN

Once they return to Adler's home, they stagger into the house. Exhaustion was coming over each one. It has been a long and challenging night. No one was saying much. Mykel heads directly for his bedroom.

"Sonya. Is it okay if I go and speak with him?" Ken asks.

"Yes." As Ken heads towards the back of the house, Sonya turns to Adelle. "Thank you so much for being there today. I am a nervous wreck." Sonya's lips were trembling.

Looking at Sonya's expression, Adelle felt she needs to say something. "Ken will get this figured out. I can't help thinking that we are all missing something."

With a quiet tapping on Mykel's bedroom door, not waiting for a reply, Ken enters. He finds Mykel hiding under his bed covers. Pulling the covers back gently, Ken starts talking to him.

"Hey. How are you doing?" Ken asks. Mykel has his face buried in his pillow so no one can hear him sobbing. In a muffled sound, Ken could barely make out his words.

"I didn't do it." Mykel mumbles.

"We all know that. Steve will take care of all of it. The video should prove you weren't there and that someone has misidentified you." Pausing as he searches for something else to say to comfort the young boy, Ken is painfully aware that the law often does not work that way. During the moments of silence, Ken can hear Mykel's tears. "It is okay to be frightened because I would be." Ken expresses his thoughts in hopes of letting Mykel know it is okay not to be alright.

To encourage Mykel, he continues. "We won't let anything happen to you, Mykel. We will do everything in our power to ensure that detective or any other detective does not bother you about this case again." Ken muscles up his sternest voice to help reassure

Mykel.

Slightly turning his head to the right, Mykel exhales and lets out an audible "Thank you."

"You are safe now. Think you can get some sleep?"

"Are you staying here? Can you?" Mykel asks. "They came and got me from my house..." Mykel's voice tappers off.

Ken could understand the question's reason but wasn't sure what Sonya would say. "Let me discuss it with your mom. Okay? Mykel, you understand that what happened today was not your fault?" Ken states in more of a lecturing tone than a true question.

Mykel does not answer. Instead, he just lays there. Ken continues. "People make mistakes. We don't know who that witness was but realize they could have thought it was you at the store or they have an alternative motive, both having nothing to do with you."

Turning over, Mykel has a look of confusion on his face. "An alternative motive?"

"Yes. They might know who robbed the store. Maybe a brother or a close friend. In a crime, someone often gives false information to completely steer the cops in another direction."

"That's wrong."

"Yes, Mykel, it is wrong. But they do it thinking they are helping their friend or themselves."

Mykel searches Ken's face for deception, but he only finds the truth. "Thanks." Mykel sits up and leans in, giving Ken a huge hug. Frozen at that moment for a few seconds; it felt good to Ken. As the embrace breaks off a little, Ken tries to reassure Mykel once more before leaving his room.

"Try to get some sleep tonight. Tomorrow is a fresh day."

"Sure thing." Mykel quips as he turns back over. "Please stay."

"I will talk with your mom." He reminds Mykel.

Mykel rolls over and turns to face the bedroom wall. Before Ken can get up, he feels a tap on his shoulder. He sees it is Adelle without fully turning his head towards her.

"I am fine. Leave me alone." He snaps at Adelle, thinking she has come in to comfort him.

Removing her hand quickly, she reminded him of something she had thought of while talking with Sonya in the living room. It was very important. "Last Wednesday was bring your child to work day, wasn't it?" She knows he would make the connection. Immediately after delivering this news to Ken, she leaves the room, closing the door behind her.

Knowing he had just made a grave error, Ken felt his heart sink into his stomach. He had no right speaking sharply to Adelle. He assumed wrong. She wasn't there to comfort him. After all, she was right. He would have to apologize, but first, he wants to give the news to Steve. He calls Steve right away so Mykel can hear.

"Hello," Steve answers.

Ken instantly begins to talk. "Last Wednesday, I brought Mykel to my workplace. It was Bring Your Child to Work day. He was with me or someone in my office all day." Speaking as fast as he could, Ken continues. "After work, we went to the hospital where his mother was. We stayed late and returned to my house, where he spent the night." After relaying his thoughts, Ken takes a breath.

"You are his alibi. Sounds to me that most of the day can be verified. I would say the police have the wrong young man."

"Not only that, hold on," Ken says as he opens his phone messages to find the company email about the work event. "I will send you the company email about it. The date matches the day of the robbery."

Holding on the phone for a minute, Ken waits for Steve's acknowledgment of the email.

"Got it. Perfect. I will call the detective right now. Call you right back."

Sitting impatiently, Ken waits to hear back from Steve. He knows he is in trouble with Adelle at this moment, but he does not want to leave Mykel's side until they hear back from Steve. He is hoping the detective answers so they have information soon. Leaving a voicemail would not help Ken's anxiety at all.

A few more minutes go by before Ken's cell phone rings. "Hello. What did he say?"

"The detective said he would make a few calls to verify this information in the morning. In the meantime, no trips anywhere, okay?"

Ken is more than happy to agree. Not wanting Mykel to worry one more second, Ken shakes his shoulder gently to get his attention. "Good news. We can prove it wasn't you." Ken announces.

Sonya enters the room as Ken tells Mykel the news. Mykel sits up as his mother reaches over to give him another strong, long hug. "I love you, little man. I love you."

"I love you too, mom. I didn't do it."

Reassuring. Ken speaks up. "We know, son. You are free."

Realizing he had not hung up the phone, Ken thanked Steve for everything he did for them. "Thank you for everything. I owe you one."

"I didn't do a thing. Anytime you need me. Just let me know." Steve ends the call. Ken gets up and goes to the living room, hoping to find Adelle. He is surprised not to find her there. Sonya comes out of Mykel's room and tells Ken, "Adelle left."

"Left? She is waiting in the car?"

"No, she left. Can you blame her?" Ken knows Sonya is right. However, it is late at night and not a good time to walk alone.

"Someone picked her up," Sonya adds.

"Who? Did she know that person?"

"I have no way of knowing, Ken. A car drove up, and she left. That is all I can tell you."

Regardless of his actions, Ken was not happy about Adelle walking out. To him, that is unacceptable behavior, especially at this hour of the night. He attempts to call her, but there is no answer. Ken follows up by sending a text with the same result. She is ignoring him. He could only hope she had called someone she knew to take her home.

Ken has always been the type who talks out a problem when it occurs. He never walks away mad, right or wrong. Adelle not answering her phone and leaving was something he would have to discuss with her right after he asked for forgiveness. After all, she would not have left if he had not snapped at her.

The day had taken its toll on Ken. He could not imagine how much the circumstances affected Mykel and his mother. At least they were together. He was happy to get them home; the case should probably be over for them.

As he leaves to go home, Sonya comes over to him. "I don't know what I would have done without you today." Giving Ken a huge bear hug, she said, "You did a good thing today. You did."

"Just glad I could be here," Ken says.

"Now you go grovel at the feet of Adelle. You owe her one heck of an apology."

"I do. I hope she can forgive me."

Sharing a little wisdom, Sonya continues, "Don't throw money at it. Flowers and candy are nice, but it doesn't get the job done. Give something of yourself. Show her with actions how much you regret those actions."

"You're right. She isn't answering my texts."

"You deserve that. Let her cool off. Talk to her tomorrow. That should give you some time to figure out how you will fix this. It would be best to let her know why you reacted that way. The scariest thing you can do is open yourself up to someone else."

"I'm in trouble.

"You are. Good luck."

He gives Sonya a peck on the forehead and heads home. Not before swinging by Adelle's place in hopes of seeing if she is up. He at least needs to know if she made it home okay. As he slows his car down while passing her house, he can see her in her living room, sitting on her couch. Stopping the car, he sits and watches her for a few moments, debating if he should knock on the door or give her some time.

Sonya was right; he thinks it through first. He doesn't know what he should say now other than how sorry he was. He should try to sleep on it. She is owed that much.

CHAPTER NINETEEN

The darkness of the night added no relief to Ken's thoughts. Searching his mind, Ken never recalls ever snapping at his wife Mel the entire time they were together. They had their disagreements, as all couples do, but he never found himself in such a state as to lash out at her. He still could not believe he had done that to Adelle.

Ken only realizes that he cannot go through the entire day before he speaks with her. And he knows he needs to do it in person. That means going by her house first thing. Sneaking a peak at the clock, he has had for years, it reads 3:17 am. Deciding to try to get more sleep if he can, he closes his eyes.

After tossing and turning for the next hour, Ken determines he should just get up. Showering and getting dressed for the day did not take as much time as he had hoped. It did not delay his travel to Adelle's house.

Parking out front, Ken walks over the front door and sits on the porch steps, using the time to figure out the right words knowing Adelle was probably still asleep. He couldn't be more wrong.

After getting her coffee, Adelle gingerly walks into the living room to watch the sunrise. But before she could do that in the morning light, she noticed Ken sitting on the first step to her porch. His arms are folded across his knees his head is lying on his arms. He looks desolate. Adelle heads for the front door and puts her coffee on the end table before opening the door.

Ken hears the front door open to his astonishment. Jumping up to face her, his heart races. He had not had time to figure out what he would say.

"I didn't mean to wake you up." Ken starts.

"I didn't sleep well last night."

Bowing his head for a moment, Ken knew all too well it was his fault. "I came to apologize to you." Looking back at Adelle, he notices she is leaning on the door frame with her hands crossed. She stares back at him, showing no resolve to his opening lines.

Continuing, Ken tries his best. "I am so sorry. You did not deserve my frustration. I was so worried about what Mykel was going through I worked myself into a frenzy. I thought you were coming over to calm me down, and I wanted to stay in a fighting mood."

"That's your excuse?" stated in a sharp tone; Adelle was not having any of it.

"No. No. It is not an excuse. I am a big boy. I will accept whatever my penalty is, as I want you to know how bad I feel."

"Not bad enough to buy me flowers."

Ken chuckles a little. "I was warned not to do that if I want to show you how much I mean what I say."

Adelle pushes herself away from the door frame and centers herself, clearly still blocking the door. "For the record, I prefer various wildflowers or a gorgeous arrangement of various flowers in a variety of colors."

Instantly making a mental note, Ken knows

Adelle is coming around. "I want you to know that I am embarrassed about my behavior. I am truly sorry. It won't happen again." Taking at the moment, he studies her expression. He can see her softening as a small smile comes across her lips.

"So back to the earlier statement of being a big boy." Adelle knew her first meeting for the day was at nine A. M., and it was just after four in the morning. That gave her a few hours to play with. Since Ken was the offender, she wasn't worried about when he had to be in the office.

"Are you going to work today?" she asks.

"I could call out. No big meetings today."

"Good. I need to take my shower." Adelle declares.

"Okay." Ken did not know what to do with that.

"I need a back scrubber. I think you need to do my back for me." Ken's expression changes quickly to a smirk. Adelle caught the look and knew right where his mind went.

"No, sir Ken. You are only allowed to scrub my back." Adelle instructs.

"But that's just pure torture." Ken blurts out.

"It is supposed to be a lesson. A penalty for your behavior." Adelle giggles. "The other would be me awarding you for bad behavior, young man."

"I deserve that."

Adelle moves out of the way to let Ken in and shuts the door behind him. Knowing the shower would wake her up more than any cup of coffee, she leaves it on the table and heads for her main bathroom.

Once inside, Adelle turns to face Ken as she removes her robe. Ken watches with great anticipation. Slipping her pajamas off, she lets them fall to the floor. Standing there, she can feel his eyes examining her as if she were the greatest sculpture ever created.

"Ken. You can't wash me while you are fully dressed. Take it off," she demands.

The fact that Ken had already showered this morning completely escaped him. He starts with his shoes, and he kicks them off. He unbuttons his shirt one button at a time and begins to tug the shirt free of his pants. Sliding the shirt off, he lays it over the towel rack. Then he unbuttons his pants and takes the zipper down. Pulling his pants and underwear off, he stands before her naked as the day he is born.

Adelle loves seeing the muscles in his arms and chest. Part of the male anatomy always made her feel safe because of the strength in the protection they showed her. She also notices that Ken is having a little trouble controlling his thoughts about the firmness in his body.

As she turns to step into the shower, she gives him a little reminder. "Only allowed to wash my back."

The reminder meant little to Ken, but he was obedient. "Yes, dear." He steps behind her and feels the warm water hit his upper body. Grabbing the washcloth, he suds it up with soap and begins at her shoulders.

Adelle realizes that she might break her promise and give in. There was no reason she should be denied the pleasure of being with Ken. She just didn't want to reinforce bad behavior. As he gets to her lower back, she becomes a lost cause. And as he reached her bottom, all bets were off. She no longer cares about the penalty, except she was in the mood, and so was he.

Before they knew it, Adelle's alarm on her phone was pinging. They had both fallen fast asleep after releasing all their stress and anxiety over the previous day's events. Adelle reaches over and turns off her alarm. Ken shuffles in bed to face her. Looking at her beauty, he needs to say it one more time. "I am so sorry about the way I spoke to you. I apologize."

"Hmmm, do you?" Adelle taunts. "Do you? Prove it."

"I will take the day off and be at your service all day." Ken offers.

Considering the suggestion, Adelle turns him down. She has a million little things to do, and she knows she can get them completed if she does them alone. With Ken, she would move slower if they even got out of bed.

"I will take a rain check. I have too much to get done today, and you, mister, will be a great distraction." Adelle admits.

"I get it. You are throwing me out." Ken laughs. He understood what she was saying. Besides, he wanted to go by Mykel's house and see how he was doing today. It was important to him. But before leaving, he needs to make one more point.

Walks up to Adelle and stands right in front of her. "Just so you are fully aware, the next time you leave somewhere we are without telling me you are going and how you are going, you will have a lot of explaining to do. Is that understood?"

Adelle had not even considered that was an issue until Ken brought it up. She had forgotten about leaving without him because she only focused on his temper. She knows he is right about that too. Ken wasn't the only one who had acted poorly that night.

"Understood."

Looking into her eyes, he could see she was embarrassed. "I talk things through. I don't play games, and I am very straightforward. And as you now know, I admit when I am wrong."

"No excuse. Just know my ex was someone I could not talk to without some kind of repercussion. I learned to walk away. It was a lot easier and often a safer choice. It is a habit I will have to break."

Ken knows she is being genuine. He would talk to her about it further at another time.

"So that you know, I did drive by to verify you made it home okay. I don't know what I would have done if I could not locate you. You would certainly get more than this little lecture when I did find you, regardless of what I had done." Ken applies his best stern look while locking eyes with Adelle.

In a meek voice, Adelle attempted to explain. "I called a car service, and they were right there. Never again. Promise."

"I appreciate that."

With that discussion over and Ken making his point, he gives Adelle a kiss and heads for Mykel's house. He is hoping he will catch him before he leaves for school.

Popping over to the Adler's home, Ken was happy to see he had arrived before Mykel left for school. Knocking on the screen door, Ken shouted inside.

"Good morning. Where is everyone?"

Mykel came running over and pushed the screen door open. Ken enters the house but gets destroyed by Mykel hugging him as tightly as possible. Ken hugs back. It was a much happier day than the day before. Mykel lets go but take Ken's hand to lead him to the kitchen table where they are having cereal for breakfast.

Sonya offers up some food, "Can I get you anything?"

Normally Ken would say no, but his stomach was already growling. "I will have what he is having." That made Mykel giggle. Turning his attention to Mykel, as Sonya retrieves a bowl and spoon for Ken, he asks Mykel how he is doing.

"Did you sleep well last night?"

"I think so." Mykel answers. Sonya cuts in.

"Are you kidding me? He sounded like a chain saw... snore...snore. I swear his bedroom door was moving back and forth each time he sucked in all the air in his room."

"Mom, that's not true." Mykel quips.

Ken and Sonya laugh. There was a lot of joy knowing the whole ordeal was over.

"Mykel, do you have any questions about what happened yesterday?"

Thinking for a moment, he did. "Why couldn't I see my mom? Why did they take me away by myself?"

Wanting to reassure him, Ken tries to explain. "That was scary, wasn't it? It's normal police procedure to separate people, so they don't have time to talk to each other and get their stories together. Even though your mom had nothing to do with the robbery, just like you, they wouldn't want her telling you what to say. That is also why I told you and the detective that you wouldn't say anything until your attorney was present."

Mykel still seems confused. It was a concept that took some time to understand. Before taking another bite of his cereal, Mykel poses another question.

"If I was innocent, why did I need an attorney?"

This question was a little more delicate and probably harder for Mykel to understand. "It doesn't matter if you are innocent or guilty; one should always have an attorney present. Police have tactics to get what they want. An attorney guides you through the process."

"Oh, I think I understand." Picking up his bowl, Mykel drinks the remaining milk directly from his bowl. Being in a silly mood, Ken copies Mykel and does the same thing.

"You young men need to learn table manners," Sonya states while laughing at the two. "Little man, go finish getting ready for school."

"Yes. Mom. Ken, can you drive me?"

"Certainly. It would be my honor."

As Mykel runs to the bathroom to brush his teeth and then to his bedroom to get his backpack and put his shoes on, it gives Sonya and Ken a few minutes to talk alone.

"Again, thank you so much for being there for us."

"My pleasure. He is a great kid."

"Yes, he is." Sonya acknowledges. "You speak with Adelle?"

"I did. She made her point. Everything is good."

"Glad to hear it. You two make a cute couple." Sonya suggests. Ken's eyes widen a little bit. Many times in the past, he was told the same thing about himself and his wife. They watched as Mykel returned to the room, announcing he was ready.

"Your chariot awaits, little man." Ken smiles.

Mykel darts over to give his mother a goodbye kiss before heading to the front door.

"Behave. Come straight home after school, young man." Sonya orders. Her statement did not phase Mykel or even slow him down. He was right out the door.

"I'd better catch up," Ken says as he goes after Mykel. Once in the car, Ken has the chance to ensure that Mykel is doing well.

"Man to man, Mykel. Are you doing, okay?"

"Better. Much better."

"You know it is all right for a man to cry. We all cry at times. Things can be overpowering; sometimes, we have to let loose."

A bit mystified, Mykel asks Ken about himself. "Do you cry? Have you cried?"

"You know I do. Absolutely. Yes. We have to let our emotions out. We can't hold everything in, and sometimes that you need means to go into a room alone and cry. Stand in the shower and cry." Ken loves Mykel's, pure heart.

Mykel had taken in Ken as if Ken was his dad. That was a conversation Ken has not had with Sonya yet. He was curious about where his dad was, but it was best for him to ask her, not Mykel.

Ken wants to share the emotions he had during the ordeal. "Can I say that I was nervous? No one ever likes things happening that are out of our control. You were very brave yesterday. Do you know that?"

"I was?" Mykel asks.

Reassuring him, Ken replies. "You sure were. In any situation like that, keeping a calm head is important. You did great."

"I did that, didn't I?"

"You did. So today, if anyone asks, you say it was a misidentification, and it went no further."

Mykel didn't ask why. He knows Ken has his back, and he would do as told. "Okay. It was a mix-ident-i-faction, right?"

"Right. Remember your superpower."

"Superpower?"

"Your intelligence and compassion." Pulling up across the street from the school, Ken wants to send him off with confidence. "You are the little man your mom thinks you are."

Mykel leans in for another hug. "See you tonight?"

Ken had some football plans. "Ever hear of flag football?"

"No."

"Get some neighborhood kids together. We have a game to play."

With that, Mykel got out of the car and walked over to the crosswalk. The crossing guard stops the traffic as a small group of children heads over to the schoolyard, Mykel being one of them. Once Mykel is right in front of the school, Ken takes off for work.

CHAPTER TWENTY

Ken enters the office among the clamoring voices. Employees were in little clusters, all talking with tumultuous expressions and confusion. Ken went into his office to drop his briefcase onto his desk before returning to see what was happening. Before returning to the common area, Mr. Jenkins enters his office and closes the door behind him.

"Morning," Ken acknowledges his entrance.

"Morning. I am sad to tell you that Mr. Woodruff passed away last night."

The news was shocking to Ken. Though Mr. Woodruff was older than Ken and has been an honored Vice-President of the firm, he was too young to die, in Ken's opinion. Mr. Woodruff is the person who recruited Ken away from his previous job to work at the firm. He was like a mentor to Ken.

Upon hearing the news, he leans on his desk for support as his body loses some of its strength. It certainly wasn't the news Ken expected. Another loss in his life was going to hit him hard. After a few seconds, Ken got the nerve to ask. "How did he die? Do we know?"

"In his sleep. His wife found him this morning," explains Mr. Jenkins. "His wife told me his father also died at a relatively young age."

"I see. I never knew that."

"I don't think anyone here did." Hesitating to gather some thoughts, Mr. Jenkins continues. "That brings up two things. One, Mrs. Woodruff would like you to be a pallbearer if you are okay with that?"

"Yes. Certainly."

"Great. I will let her know. And second, Mr. Woodruff and I had already discussed making you a firm vice-president."

Ken looks up at Mr. Jenkins. Ken was stunned at the statement. He had no idea that anyone had considered him for a promotion, let alone Vice-President.

Revising the conversation, Mr. Jenkins feels compelled to explain further. "I realize it is awkward timing to be telling you this. I am because we want you to know this promotion has nothing to do with the timing of his death. You earned this promotion. We plan to tell you tomorrow during our meeting. I think it is better that you know it now."

Lingering in thought, it was a lot for Ken to take in at once. Ken feels gloom returning as if the edges of darkness were closing in on him.

"No. I understand. Thank you so much for telling me. I am honored."

"I know he wanted to tell you himself. He always saw you as his son." This statement from Mr. Jenkins reminds Ken of a conversation Ken had with Mr. Woodruff over a year ago after his family died. Warm and very lovingly, Mr. Woodruff offered all his assistance in helping Ken. He recalls his exact words, '*I never was blessed with children. I see you as the son I was supposed to have.'*

His first instinct is to reach out to Adelle. He desperately needs to reach out to someone to share his despair. "Adelle. Hi. Sorry to call you so quickly. I know you have a lot to do today. Do you have a moment?"

Adelle could hear in his voice a desperate need to talk about something. "Always."

Ken slowly tells Adelle about the Mr. Woodruff news and a little bit about their relationship over the years. He wasn't in the mood to speak about the promotion. Adelle could sense his grief through the phone.

"I am so sorry to hear that. Did your wife know him?" Adelle's question caught Ken off guard a tad, but he answered anyway.

"Yes. She simply loved him. She went to many company dinners or events and spent time with him every chance."

"She will be there to meet him. Help him cross over. Did you ask her?"

That last question perplexed Ken. "Ask who?"

"Ask your wife to help him cross over," asks Adelle

"I don't talk to her like that."

"No. You don't go to her grave and talk to her?"

Remembering his most recent visit, he knows he does. "I do. I talk to her there."

"Then why not right now?"

Considering the question, Ken wasn't sure how to answer her. "I guess it feels funny to be talking to her. She is not here."

"But she is Ken. You can feel her. Did she talk to you at the cemetery?"

"Not like a voice." Thinking Adelle was off the mark, he continued. "I don't know what I believe."

"Did you ask her anything? Get any signals?"

Reflecting, he did get an acknowledgment of their conversation. "Mel sent two gorgeous birds to me." Being very rational about life, Ken still found talking to the dead unusual. Adelle was making some great points, though. Ken wondered. "What do I say?"

"Just ask her to help Mr. Woodruff. She already knows how you feel. You can do that right now."

"Okay. Let me try it." Ken mutters.

"Call me back if you need to, okay?" Adelle offers.

"Thanks." Upon hanging up the call, Ken meditates for a few moments, thinking about what to say. Turning away from his office interior window so no one sees him talking to himself, he concentrates on the view outside his large office window.

"Hi, Mel. God, am I missing you. Someone suggested I talk with you even though you are elsewhere." Taking in another deep breath, he continues. "You might already know that Mr. Woodruff passed away last night. Can you be there to help him..." Ken takes a moment and searches for the words. "Cross over? He would like that."

Ken starts feeling a little foolish talking to Mel without her being there. "I feel a little ridiculous right now talking to no one. I pray you can hear me. Maybe I need to ask this of you at the cem…" Ken cut off his own words as he could not believe his eyes. Two birds softly settle on the edge of his picture window facing him. It appears as if it is the exact two birds from the cemetery. Sitting in awe, he just studies them, realizing this could be Mel's indication she was listening to him. Far from understanding what was happening, the one thing Ken knows is that it was no coincidence.

Sending a quick text to Adelle, Ken was starting to be in a better place. "Thanks for the suggestion. Up for some flag football tonight?" Ken realized she might read that the wrong way after a second. Quickly following it up with "Going to have a game with Mykel and his friends after work."

Adelle replied. "Only if you know, you will not win, and you can handle it, big boy."

That makes Ken laugh. "Give it your best shot. I'll pick you up at four-thirty. Better come up with a great prize for me."

"Oh, I think I know one or two. But again, I am going to win."

Something about Adelle turns Ken's whole day into one where it's a joy to be alive, even though the loss of Mr. Woodruff was hard to take and so unexpected. After gathering some information from Mr. Jenkins, Ken started calling clients to tell them the news. He also took the time to phone Mrs. Woodruff and offered to help her in any way he could.

After making endless calls, Ken calls it quits for the day. Heading to a sporting goods store, Ken picks up the flag football supplies and a few glasses of water for everyone. He had not played the game himself since his school days. He was certainly looking forward to the game. And now Adelle has made it more of a contest.

Heading to her house, he pulls up in her driveway to see her sitting on the porch. Popping up, she heads over to his car. Immediately Ken notices that she is wearing a football jersey.

"Good afternoon. You are into the Broncos?"

"Yes. I. Am." She states clearly as she slides into his passenger seat.

"But you don't live there." Ken declares.

"What? Do you have to live where your favorite team plays? Is that a rule? And who says I never did?" That kicks off Ken's mind about what he knows about Adelle. Maybe he needs to ask more questions.

"Well, did you?"

"I went to college there. Yep. I love football."

"Am I in trouble?" says Ken as he backs out of the driveway and heads to Mykel's place.

"If you are asking, do I know how to play? I do. And again. I will win."

"About that, young lady. What are we playing for?"

"A weekend of fun," Adelle suggests with a twinkle in her eye.

"A whole weekend? What are you going to do for me during that weekend."

Adelle bursts out in a loud "Ha," and laughs. "You mean what do I expect from you that weekend? Remember, I am going to win. You will be mine."

Having never met someone so playful in his

life, Ken almost planned on losing to discover her intentions. Then he thought better of it. She could tell if he didn't give it his best.

As they pull up in front of Mykel's house, they see several children waiting for them. Ken looks over at Adelle and adds some fuel to the fire. "You are going down." The phrase, though, backfired and only confirmed Adelle's resilience.

"Hi, everyone. Who do we have here?" Ken says as he opens the trunk of his car and pulls out the items for the game. He begins to walk over and notices two young girls in the group. He is pleased to see that Mykel included them in the game.

Mykel goes through all the names, which Ken knows he will never remember. As the introductions continue, adults with lounge chairs start showing up. Sonya walks out of the front door with a huge pitcher of lemonade and paper glasses.

"We can use the neighbor's yard as well," Sonya suggests as she points to her right. The two lawns are back up to each other, with the driveways on the outside of both lawns. Together makes a wide patch of grass. The parents lined up on the sidewalk with their chairs and even a couple of umbrellas. This game was now a neighborhood event. Ken had no idea how much the families loved his idea, as they all wanted to be a part of it.

"Hi, everyone. I am Ken. This is Adelle. She thinks she and her team are going to win. One can dream." The parents all laugh at Ken's comments. Adelle just shakes her head. Her brothers never made the game easy on her, and it was never flag football at home. She was ready for it.

"Okay. Who are our team captains?" Ken asks the children. Mykel steps up. And then Conrad steps forward. "Alright, Mykel and Conrad. I am going to flip a coin to see who picks first. Conrad, heads, or tails?"

"Heads." With little effort, Ken flips a quarter into the air, steps back and lets it fall to the ground. "Tails," declares Ken. Picking up the coin, Ken heads over to where all the other children are standing. He motions Adelle to follow.

"Okay, Mykel, you get the first choice," Ken says.

"You," Mykel states as he points at Ken.

Conrad chooses Adelle as they go back and forth, choosing between the children. Adelle was happy to see that the two girls were not chosen last but almost at the beginning. There were an even number of children, so it was a good thing Ken invited Adelle. Ken begins to hand out the flag football belts and explains to everyone how the game works.

The captains line up their teams and meet in the middle. One more game toss. Conrad won this time and took the ball first. One of the parents yells out, "Let the games begin." With that, the action begins. There is a lot of laughter. Kids are screaming like crazy. Everyone was having a great time when a police car pulled up.

Both officers leave their cars and walk over to see what is happening. Ken tells the children to keep playing. "We are only down 3 points. We have to win." Adelle yells to Ken, "Told you that you are going down."

With that, they line up again. Sammie snaps the ball to Mykel, who throws it to Ken. Using his height, he pushes through the children heading to the fake goalposts.

"Snap." His flag was torn off his belt. Turning around to see who got to him stood Adelle. "I warned you." She reminds him.

"Hey, looks like you are short two players. Mind if we join in?" One officer asks.

Adelle replies, "Are you any good?"

With that comment, the officers call into the station, remove their gun belts, place them into their law enforcement vehicle, and come over to play. Ken tells Mykel and Conrad to pick one for their team, and the game resumes.

The neighborhood crowd was developing. Several people have their phones out and are recording the game and posting on the internet. Before they knew it, the local TV station had shown up and started a story on the game due to the officers' involvement. It was becoming quite the scene. The little neighborhood game was anything but. All the commotion never even bothered any of the players. They all just kept playing.

Now Mykel's team was up four points, having made a touchdown.

Conrad's team has the ball back. This was their last chance to win. They line up with Adelle on the outside. The center snaps the ball, and Conrad goes back. Anticipating the play, Ken stays towards the back as well. Adelle runs around the opposing team and turns to face Conrad. He throws the football. As it soars through the air, Ken cuts Adelle off and reaches for the ball. Intercepting it, he runs forward. Adelle grabs for a flag and misses. In hot pursuit, she runs after him and, in a full-on tackle, takes Ken down from the back. The ball gets loose on his way down, and Conrad is right there. Grabbing the ball in mid-air, he runs for their endzone. First to the left, then shifting around the children to the right. As he gets to the endzone, he spikes the ball into the ground and does a victory dance.

The parents are all on their feet, yelling and cheering. Adelle and Ken are still on the ground but watch Conrad dance before Ken speaks up.

"Officers. Can you arrest this young lad? That

tackle was illegal." One officer walks over and looks down at the two.

"It was illegal. But you two are the adults here. Get up. You are both under arrest for an illegal play."

"Both?" Ken pleads. The officers start laughing as everyone joins in. As he stands up, Ken's face still has dirt and grass. "That was unfair." No one cares but Ken.

As the local station starts interviewing the children, Ken figures it is a good time to sneak away before the cameras turn on them. The last thing Ken was interested in was the limelight. After all, it was supposed to be a small game with Mykel and his friends. Nothing more.

Slipping quietly into the car, Ken and Adelle slowly move his car out to the street, put it in drive and leave. Once on the road, Ken has a bone to pick with Adelle. "Cheaters do not win."

"Well, we did win. You belong to me all weekend." Adelle states with confidence.

"Wrong. It was flag football, and you tackled me after missing my flag." Ken fortifies his stance.

Adelle knows she cheated, but what fun would it be not to have a winner? She suggests, "We can flip for it." Ken shoots over a look of playful disappointment to Adelle.

CHAPTER TWENTY-ONE

The following day Ken arrives back at Mykel's house to see how everything is going. Sonya answers the door. "Where did you two run off to yesterday? The press wanted to interview you. You're our local hero."

"I'm no hero. It was supposed to be a friendly little game. How did the news spread so fast?"

"Mykel invited everyone on the block. He was so excited. He didn't want to let you down."

"Let me down; how?" Ken asks.

"By not having enough people to play the game," Sonya explains.

"You know we could play with four people if we wanted to?" Ken comments.

"I know that. But he was so excited and wanted everyone to know the game was at his house he went a little overboard."

Right then, Mykel darts out of his room. "Thought I heard you. That game was great. Too bad we lost."

"Do you think we lost? Adelle pulled a very illegal move to get that win. Cheaters can't win."

"They do all the time," Mykel spoke as if he was an adult. He was right, they do, but Ken wasn't about to give in to the loss.

"Then I suggest a replay." Ken offers up.

"Not tonight. Mykel has homework he did not do yesterday." Sonya reminds Mykel.

"Can you help me?" Mykel asks Ken.

"Sure. If it is okay with your mother."

Smiling, Sonya replies, "Be my guest."

Going over to the coffee table in the middle of the living room, Mykel sits by his book he already has open and his notebook paper. His backpack is flung on the couch. Ken sits beside Mykel on the floor with his back against the couch.

"What are we studying?"

"Math. Not my best subject." Mykel quips.

"You are in luck. It is one of mine. I use it a lot."

"For what?"

"We don't just draw buildings. We must know the space's square footage, the building's height, and everything else about the building, which requires math."

From there, they dove into Mykel's homework as Sonya listened in. Ken has a way of teaching, and Mykel understood everything Ken was telling him. Ken's special knack was taking one of Mykel's math problems and changing it to something Mykel could relate to. Many times, Ken would use football analogies to make his point. Sonya knew he would have been a great father or teacher had he decided to go that route.

After completing Mykel's homework, Ken and Mykel continued to talk. Mykel was having a little trouble at school with another student. The student was causing problems with more than just Mykel. "He is just so mean to everyone. He is a bully." Mykel explains.

Ken gives some advice. "You know what that could mean, don't you?" Mykel shakes his head no before Ken continues. "Bullies are often people who feel very insecure or whose family life isn't all that good." Ken could tell Mykel did not fully understand. Ken tries to explain further. "In other words, his home life is probably not good. He may not get all the love you get from your mom, from his parents."

Something clicks for Mykel. "He only has his dad. He is drunk a lot."

"Well, that sounds like this young man doesn't have the greatest home life and is lashing out some. Does he have any close friends?" Ken knew the answer but wanted Mykel to think it through.

"No. Not really. People are afraid of him. Brian is also kind of big for his age."

Ken explains in a little more detail what is taking place while being very cautious of his wording. He did not want to make any assumptions about what was happening in that young man's home. Ken steers the conversation to how Mykel can choose to ignore the bully or how he could handle him the next time he comes after Mykel, giving Mykel options.

"You know he probably doesn't have a lot of friends."

"Just one I know of," Mykel replies

"What makes you think they are friends?"

"They are always together."

"That doesn't make them friends. Friends share information. Have each other's back. They are there for each other. Is that what you see going on there?"

"No. I think Darryl just hangs with him, so he is not picked on."

"Good observation Mykel."

Still intently listening to the discussion, Sonya never interferes. Ken is right on track. She would be telling Mykel the same information. Ken and Sonya found the questions Mykel keeps asking mature and considerate of the situation.

The previous night's discussion could not have been timed any better. The next day, Mykel is confronted by the bully he had mentioned to Ken. Though he had not had enough time to decide how to handle his net encounter, Mykel quickly chose what he wanted to do.

Brian taunts Mykel. "Hey, little My – Kel," The bully says as he starts to approach Mykel. Making fun of others' names was one of the bully's trademarks. Mykel turns around to face him.

"Brian. There you are. I have a question for you." Mykel's comment throws Brian off his game. Mykel continues before Brian can fully react. "Hear about our football game the other day? Well, we want a rematch. I was wondering if you would join us?" Brian was dumbfounded.

"Why a rematch?" Brian asks.

"Because the other team cheated. Will you join us? I can let you know when as soon as we figure it out. We need one more person besides you. Know of anyone you want to join us?"

Brian had no idea what was going on. No one had ever invited him to participate in anything. He already knew his bully attitude was blown. "How about Darryl?"

"Darryl. Yeah, ask him. He would be great." With that, Mykel walks into class without any trouble. Mykel couldn't wait to get home and tell his mother the news.

Ken was busy at the office. The top executives encouraged Ken to move into Mr. Woodruff's old office, but Ken felt it was too soon. Instead, he prefers to work with Morgan to flush out the details of the new building. It took a few hours to get everything lined up. All the little details were in place, and the full proposal was ready. Ken hands it over to Morgan to handle. His promotion had come through, and Ken knew he was turning over his office to Morgan.

That only added a little pressure for Ken to move. He didn't have many personal items in his office at all. One picture of a beach in Hawaii hung on the wall. It was one of the first things he put in his office when he was promoted years before. It always reminds him of his honeymoon with Mel. Before everything happened, Ken would have left the picture behind. But now he finds himself talking to Mel from time to time.

Lifting it off the wall, he feels it is best to be the first thing he puts in his new office. Carrying it over, he opens the office door. Ken was not ready to see that many of Woodruff's items were already gone. Over in the far corner was a fancy globe perched on a solid oak frame. The oceans were made from blue lapis, while some major cities were marked with gemstones. Ken always loved the globe and was very surprised it was still there. Figuring someone would be coming to get it later, he hung his picture on the wall across from his new desk. There had been a picture there before. The hook was still in the wall. His picture was a little larger than the one there before. It was good because the wall showed signs of dirt, leaving an outline of the previous picture frame. Ken's image covered it up.

"Ah, good, Ken, you are moving in." Mr. Jenkins comments. He had been walking by the office and saw Ken inside.

"Morgan needs a place to work. When will they pick up the globe?" Ken asks.

"Knowing you love that thing, he left it to you."

"I can't accept that." Ken contends.

"Well, it's yours. Enjoy." Mr. Jenkins leaves the room as Ken heads over to the globe. He had always had the urge to spin the hell out of it but never did. He was afraid Mr. Woodruff would have thought he was being silly. Nothing was stopping him now. Reaching for the globe, Ken gives it a hard push and steps back, watching it spin. The moment wasn't lost on him. His own life had been spinning until recently.

Without waiting for it to stop, Ken heads back to his old office to grab his last box, which he filled with his drawing tools, books, and a couple of potted plants. Woodruff's previous assistant had entered Ken's new office in the meantime and caught a glimpse of the globe spinning. Standing there for a moment to watch it spin, Ken re-enters the office without a word.

"You know, I always wanted to do that." The assistant states before leaving.

Calling out behind her, Ken makes a suggestion. "You can spin it anytime you want." She was now going to be his assistant. She has always been good at her job. He knew he was lucky to have her assigned him since this new position would come with new duties, and she understood what was needed. He was going to have to rely on her.

His new desk was almost three times bigger than his previous desk. It was made of solid oak and held a maroon-colored leather desktop, a gold-plated desk lamp, and a fancy pen and pencil holder. No calendar. Ken would have to get used to someone else maintaining his calendar now. That would take some getting used to.

The high-back leather chair matches the leather top on the desk. It shows only a little wear and tears on the arms of the chair. Walking over to it, he sits down slowly and gently rubs his hands on the worn section. The same place Mr. Woodruff had run his hands as well. Being uneasy sitting in the chair, he finds himself shifting before he can no longer handle being in that seat. Ken stands up.

Walking over to the huge picture window with

an opposite view from his previous office, he takes in the new viewpoint. The window faces the high rises in Chicago. Just beyond the skyline is the great lake. Ken starts to remember the many times he had been there but sitting on the other side of the desk. Strolling over to that side of the desk, he sits where he had many times before observing Mr. Woodruff's empty chair.

He says, "Mel, I remember coming here to tell Mr. Woodruff that you accepted my proposal. He was so excited." Ken drops his head for a moment as he realizes many of his life stories are in this office.

"And again, when I told him you...we were pregnant." Suddenly Ken recalls a detail he had forgotten all about. "Mel, he set up a college fund for our Clint. I for...got. I completely forgot." Swirling in his brain, he realizes the fund is still active. "What do we do with it, Mel? Mykel can use it. Do we give it to Mykel? Would you and Clint be okay with that?" Darting eyes with a look of bewilderment takes over Ken's expression. Quickly he turns to look at the window. Would the birds confirm his question? He waits, sitting there silently in a rigid position. Would they come?

Nothing. "Mel, is that not the right thing to do?" he begs for confirmation.

His new assistant walks into the office with the day's mail. "I believe Mr. Hines, you should be sitting in the other chair." Ken makes eye contact with her.

"You're right. Ken. No, Mr. Hines, please. Never feels comfortable to me."

"Yes. Ken, it is. Here is the morning mail." She hands the mail directly to Ken as he rises and walks back around the desk. She had already used the letter opener on the envelopes, and all in-office correspondence was in a folder. All his years at the firm, he had opened his mail.

"By the way. You are trending."

"I'm trending?" Ken looks at her in wonder.

"Yep." She pulls her cell phone from her pocket and scrolls for a second. "Here you go," she says as she hands him her phone. The front-yard football game from a few days earlier is on the screen. As he watches it, he focuses on the smiles on everyone's faces. It was a nice reminder of how fun that day was.

"There's another one. Hold on." The assistant takes back the phone, scrolls, and hands it back. Now there is the footage of the police officers joining in posted by the police department.

Handing the phone back to her, Ken is shocked, "Two million views? Who is watching this stuff?

"Better question, who isn't?" Smiling as she walks out the door. Ken had known the local news had aired the footage but never thought about the internet.

Turning his attention back to the mail, he opens the first envelope. Ken instantly knew it was a card. As he pulls it out slowly, his eyes focus on the image. He is stunned. It is an image of two beautiful blue birds facing each other as they both sit on the branch of a tree that appears as if they are nuzzling their beaks together. For Ken, this confirmation was imperative. As a natural expression of the emotion surging inside, Ken unconsciously places his hand on his heart and leaves it there for a few seconds while breathing a little heavier than usual. In a whispering voice, Ken speaks aloud, "Thank you."

Having some free open time on his schedule before everyone realizes they can come to him for work issues, he knows he has some free time on his hands. Firing up the computer on the desk, Ken begins a search. Looking up Shadow Drive on a map, he zooms out. Then he sees a large green patch just a few blocks away from the Adler's home. Looking up the park, he quickly calls the facilities department. He's going to borrow the company transportation van for the weekend.

CHAPTER TWENTY-TWO

Saturday finally came as Ken and Adelle rolled up in the firm's transportation van. Adler's front lawn was full of children. It was most of the children from the football game two weeks earlier. Connor's dad brought his truck for all the chairs and umbrellas. Along with a few coolers of soft drinks.

The children all hustle into the van, along with some adults. Once everyone is packed up, Ken drives to the neighboring park. The facility coordinator waits for them to arrive and watches as they all step out of the van. Since many local track and field events were held at this park, it would not attract as much attention as the last game.

Mykel and his mother, Sonya, never knew a football-type field existed. It wasn't 100 yards, but it would do the trick. Ken also reserved the picnic shelter right next to the field. Everyone started to unload the chairs and coolers. A couple of dads start up the barbecue pit while other parents arrive.

Ken starts handing out the flag belts when he sees Mykel running over to meet two boys. Excited, Mykel brings them over to Ken. "This is Brian, and this is Darryl" Turning to Ken, Mykel introduces Ken, "This is my new dad." Ken was not about to correct Mykel but made a note to talk with him later.

"Well, hello, Brian and Darryl. It is a pleasure to make your acquaintance." Shaking both of their hands, he continues to ask questions. "Will you be playing with us today?" Ken recognizes the names. With pride, he makes eye contact with Mykel to let him know he did well.

Both boys shook their heads yes. "Here you go." Ken offers them both their belts.

"Alright, everyone. Gather over here." Ken calls out to all the children as he motions to come around. "Okay, for those who did not participate in the last game, know this is a repeated game. Tackling someone,"

Ken looks over at Adelle as he continues, "will not be tolerated."

"Why are you looking at me?" Adelle complains.

Ken laughs as he continues with all the instructions. "Okay, Mykel. Sammie. Mykel heads or tails?"

"Heads."

Flipping the quarter into the air, it comes up heads. "Mykel, you get a first-player pick."

Sammie and Mykel pick the same teammates, except Brian and Darryl. Mykel purposely picks Brian for his team. He remembers Ken's words about not having real friends. Just maybe, today, things will change.

"Okay, does everyone understand the rules?" Ken asks

Mykel looks at Adelle and mouths the words, "No... tackling." Pointing to her ear, she returns the sentiment, mouthing, "I can't hear you."

The teams line up, and Mykel is ready. "Ready...

Position...Blue 42" The ball is snapped, and the game is on its way. Mykel gives Brian the ball. Being the former bully, he runs right through the team. Everyone seems to be afraid to even get near him.

Jumping up and down, Mykel yells, "Touchdown. We got a touchdown."

Knowing the circumstances as to why Brian was invited to the game, Ken decides he needs to have a quick talk with Mykel. Pulling him aside for a minute, Ken looks into Mykel's eye to see his reaction to what he is about to say. "I have to ask. Did you give the ball to Brian, knowing no one would touch him?"

Shaking his head, no. "No. I wanted him to be part of the game from the start." Searching Mykel's eyes, Ken feels he is telling the truth.

"Next play?"

"When we get the ball back, it will be someone else." Padding Mykel back to let him know he fully appreciates Mykel's actions.

Sammie's team now has the ball. Lining up, Sammie is about to return the favor. "Ready, 12, 13,

Green 19." The ball is snapped. Sammie gets it as everyone runs forward. One team member runs by Sammie as he fakes the ball to him. Then, with great effort, Sammie passes the ball to Darryl, who has run halfway down the small field. Leaping into the air, Darryl catches the ball and runs towards the goal line.

An opposing team player pulls Darryl's flag two yards from the end zone. The game is picking up steam. Signaling his team, Sammie runs down the field and gets the team to line up.

Just as the team lines up, two teammates start laughing. Right there on the field is a squirrel who appears as if he has lined up with Mykel's team. Everyone stops to look at the furry creature. It begins to run towards Sammie's team as the boys and girls start to run out of its path. But the squirrel has other plans and turns immediately, following some team members. Shouts and screams are coming from previously manly football players, who now sound like little kids seeing a spider. The adults break out in laughter, watching as the silliness takes place.

The little brown squirrel seems insistent on torturing the kids on the field as if to say *stay away from my tree.* The commotion drew the attention of other people enjoying the park. Mykel looks at Brian and nods as if to say, "we can chase this squirrel away."

"Let's go," yells Mykel as he and Brian begin to run toward the squirrel. Other teammates join in on the chase. "You guys go to the right; we will go to the left and steer him back to the tree." Brian instructions.

The two teams are now in hot pursuit of an innocent little creature defending his territory. Blocking every turn the little squirrel makes, he finally settles on running back up the tree to a safe distance. The children all high-fived each other for a job well done.

With that break, everyone decides to call it half-time. Heading to the sidelines and their parents, they refresh themselves with water and a few munchies. Then it is time to go again. All the children head to their previous spots, with Sammie hoping for a touchdown.

Lining back up, the teams are ready to continue.

With only two yards to go, Sammie calls it off, "Ready, 12, 13, Green 19." Once the ball is snapped, Sammie pretends to lob the ball over to Darryl again but instead does a quick turn and tosses the ball to Cindy. Sammie had been watching the plays during the first half of the game and noticed the boys were playing around the girls no matter which team they were on. Using that fact, Cindy ran the ball into the end zone. Sammie's team cheers and rushes over to their player, putting her on their shoulders.

"Not to worry. We are taking it back. You haven't won yet!!" Mykel reminds the opposing team. Running to line up again and Mykel's team having the ball, he calls out, "Ready...hike...hike....Blue 42". Center passes the ball to Mykel, who tosses it over to Ken. Ken takes off running. Adelle positions herself right in front of him. Making a quick rollout move, Ken slips passed Adelle and he half expects her to tackle him again. He was so focused on her he did not see Darryl come up on his other side and pull his flag off.

"What?" Ken exclaims

"You're down," Darryl announces.

"Everyone over here," Mykel calls out. Once in the huddle, the little man reprimands Ken. "If you didn't pay so much attention to her, you could have made a touchdown." Mykel's honesty is refreshing to Ken. The other boys wait for a moment to see Ken's reaction before they all start laughing.

"Yes, sir." Ken acknowledges his misstep."

After giving the team the next play, they break and line up again. "Ready... hike...Blue 42". Catching the opposing team off guard by shortening the call, Mykel gives the ball to Brian, who runs it into the end zone.

"Touchdown" yells Brian.

"Way to go," and applause is heard from the teams. Looking over Mykel, Ken and Adelle realize the applause is coming from the detective that wanted to arrest Mykel earlier. Immediately Ken's body tenses up as he heads over to see why the detective is there.

The detective can see Ken is already in defensive mode and walking with the intent to cut the detective off from getting anywhere near Mykel. Mykel's mother sees Ken's focus and turns around to see the detective standing on the sideline.

Before Ken reaches the detective, he throws up his hands. "Everything is good." To calm Ken down, he continues speaking quickly to get the information out. "I went by the house, and no one was there. A neighbor told me you were all here."

Ken was now standing only a foot away from the detective. He let him continue speaking but was still cautious about whatever the detective said.

"I wanted to come by and let you know everything has checked out for Mykel. We have apprehended the boy who committed the burglary. He looks a lot like Mykel. I can see a certain resemblance. I just wanted him to know there was no ill intent. But we have to follow all leads until a case is solved."

Ken knew that. He also knew these words would help Mykel through the ordeal. They would help him to leave it behind. "Mykel, can you come over here for a second."

Trusting Ken, Mykel comes over as his mother

joins him.

"Hi, Mykel. I am sure you remember me. I wanted to let you know we are sorry for all the drama the other night. We did catch the boy who did the deed. I want you to know you were strong and brave. We need more young men like you." The officer offers up.

Looking at Mykel, Ken urges him to reply. "Mykel, do you have anything to say?'

"This means no one will come and take me out of my house again?"

The detective understood the fear behind the whole experience. "Yes. This is over with. Closed."

"Thank you."

"You any good?" Ken wisecracks.

"What?" The detective is a little confused.

"Mykel, the detective, will take my place in the next play." Ken turns and looks at him and smiles. Feeling a little cornered into playing, he takes off his suit jacket and heads into the game for a play.

Sitting on the sideline next to Sonya, Ken

enjoyed being a cheerleader for a couple of plays. With the score tied and Ken's bet with Adelle hanging in the balance. Ken takes up his position again. He is determined to win.

Mykel's team has the ball. Ken suggests a field kick, "As we only need three points, and no one has said we can't do that." The huddle all agrees. Everyone decides Pam should kick the ball. She often plays soccer with her older brothers, and the opposing team would not expect it.

"Ready...do it...Blue 42". The ball is snapped. Mykel takes one knee and positions the ball for the kick. Pam runs back and sets up for the kick. She takes her step, and her foot lifts the ball into the air. It sails over the opposing team. In unison, the team yells, "Field Goal."

"No. Illegal." yelled some of Sammie's teammates.

"No, it's not." Mykel states.

"No one said we could kick the ball." They confront Mykel's team.

"No one said we couldn't!" Mykel explains. "We win. We win." Sammie's team concedes as the heat of the day is stealing whatever energy they have left. Retiring to the sidelines, the children grab their drinks and snacks while hitting the ground—a couple of boys sprawl out on the grass in total exhaustion.

As Ken puts his arm around Adelle, he cannot help but grin. "Seems like I win the bet."

Adelle smiles back. "I am not convinced that was legal in flag football."

"Oh, it is legal. Look it up."

"Fine. You better be nice to me." Adelle warns.

"I am always nice to you, Ms. Rayne."

CHAPTER TWENTY-THREE

Not waiting for a holiday weekend, Ken had decided to take a couple of days off to spend the weekend he promised Adelle. Adelle had arranged her projects so that she could escape the city with Ken for the entire four days.

It was a relatively short drive to the resort, under two hours. The drive was full of teasing and get-to-know-you games.

"Alright, Ken, what has been your most embarrassing moment?" Adelle asks.

"Going for the jugular. I see...Let me think." Searching his mind, Ken wasn't sure. Thinking for a few minutes, Ken was quiet.

"Come on. It is un-human to have none." Adelle jibes.

"It isn't that I don't have one; I am trying to figure out which one is more embarrassing. It's either going to work on a Saturday and thinking it's a Friday and not even realizing why there's so little traffic ooorrrr," and dwelling on the last word before starting again "...ripping your pants at a wedding while dancing and not even making crazy moves. You pick."

Adelle laughs.

"Your turn, missy." Ken says.

"I was walking into an office when my high heel caught on the rug. I went down like a ton of bricks. Because of the office partitions, I was there, and then I wasn't. I fell right behind them." Adelle says, laughing through her explanation.

"Like Sandra Bullock in that movie." Ken offers.

"Not that glamorous. She stayed up walking. I did not." Still laughing as she recalls the ordeal.
"I will have you know I popped right back up like the energizer bunny."

Laughing so hard, Ken had tears coming out of his eyes, and he worried about staying in the car lane.

"Yours sounds so much better than mine."

As soon as they can both breathe again, Adelle continues her line of questioning. "Next one. Did you have a childhood nickname? And what was it?"

"Oh geez. It was Tater. Because I loved tater tots growing up. I asked my mom for them every night."

"Tater? Okay, Tater." Adelle jokes. Ken shoots her a look and then goes after her.

"Your turn again."

"Ugh. Twinkle toes because I walked on my toes first for probably the first three months."

"I'll take my Tater to your twinkle and raise you five." Ken had no idea what that meant but thought it was clever.

Ken decides to take the lead, "If you had a warning label, what would it say?"

Adelle had never thought about that. "Let me think. Warning label." A small grin starts to appear on her face. "Crossing her could lead to an early death."

"Wow. Deadly." Ken responds.

"Yours?"

A very mischievous grin came across Ken's face. "Warning. Contains nuts." Busting out in laughter again, Adelle finally gets out her thoughts. "I hope so."

"I didn't mean those. I meant I am nutty. A little crazy. And you are about to find out just how much." It is a gentle reminder that Adelle's team lost the game, and Ken won the bet.

The timing could not have been more perfect as they pulled up to the resort. It is a beautiful setting with a large a-frame wooden building. Adelle can see off to the right where a large lake surface sparkles in the sun just as it is starting to surrender to the water. There are several small boats tied to the makeshift dock. Immediately Adelle had plans to be on one of them.

Pulling up to the entrance, they park the car and enter the lobby. It is spacious with large comfy blue chairs. A center fireplace is lit, adding to the feeling of being miles out of town. The resort reminds her of a place she had previously stayed in the Grand Tetons years ago. She never knew this place was so close to home.

"Adelle, over here." Waiting for her to walk over to the front desk, he begins to ask a couple of questions. "I know I am in charge of the weekend," he says with a wink, "I have booked us dinner reservations for tonight. And how about a couple of massages tomorrow?"

"That sounds great. Can we get a boat ride in as well?"

"Sure. How about Sunday?" Ken asks the front clerk.

"Yes, we have several boats available Sunday. Do you need a skipper, or do you want to pilot the boat yourselves?" The clerk asks.

"I can skipper it." Ken decides. If they could find a nice secret cove, they might have some other fun too.

"Do you want to have food prepared and on the boat for you?"

"Oh yes," Adelle speaks up as she reaches for the menu the clerk hands her.

"You can call the front desk later tonight to let

them know what you would like."

"Nice. I do want to look it over a little."

Being able to treat someone to fun and enjoyment was something Ken did love to do. He worked to earn money his whole life only to spoil others with it. He misses having someone to show how much they mean to him. It hit him like lightning. *"Am I falling in love?"* Ken wonders to himself. They haven't spoken of the "L" word yet, but Ken could feel it was moving to the tip of his tongue.

Getting to their room, Adelle was again in awe. It has a large, fluffy bed with white linens, a bluish-green comforter, and matching pillows. The couch across from the big-screen TV was also sage-colored with white pillows. But the view from the three large windows caught Adelle's attention.

They could see the lake as some people were on their boats having a nice evening float. The rolling hills that surround the resort are covered in bright green trees. She could see several paved walking paths, and the hope of having an evening stroll shot to the top of her list.

"They have a large indoor pool encircled with large picture windows." Ken submits. "Hope you brought your bathing suit."

As Adelle turns around, Ken sees that she is beaming with happiness. "I did." Facing Ken, she now sees into the bathroom and notices the huge spa tub. "That thing is big enough for two people."

"We have a couple of hours to kill before dinner." Ken implies they should be testing it out. Not even unpacking, Adelle takes the hint. Sliding off her shoes where she stands, she starts to move towards the bathroom. Next was her blouse and bra falling to the floor. Ken watches in anticipation. Just as she stands within the door frame, she drops her pants and underwear, giving Ken a show.

Ken follows earnestly. Kicking off his shoes, removing his pants, and pulling off his shirt with one tug. Soon they are both facing each other in the warm water.

"We have to stop bathing like this." Ken jokes.

"Never." Adelle lets her foot slip right where she planned on placing it. Quickly they find themselves working up an appetite. A couple of times, Adelle worried about the sounds they were making being heard by a neighboring room, but that fear gave way swiftly to the pleasure they were both experiencing.

Those few hours flew by. Next thing they knew, they were getting a little fancy for dinner. They were ready for a feast by descending the stairs to the lobby and into the elegant dining room. White linen tablecloths, candles, and cherry-wood chairs added to the adventure Adelle felt she was on.

Ken made all the gentlemanly gestures, from pulling out her chair to choosing the wine, smelling the cork, and ordering her food. *"Have I found my knight in shining armor?"* she thinks, convincing herself. Her mother had always warned her about having romantic fantasies. She would say, "remember, no one is perfect." Mom's voice echoes in her brain. She didn't want to ruin the night and pushed the thought to the farthest part of her mind.

"Can we go for a little walk?" Adelle asks Ken since they have finished dinner.

"That would be nice."

It was driving Adelle crazy. Since she had first laid eyes on the place when they pulled up, she wondered if Ken had been here before. She was unsure how to approach the topic, walking in silence and listening to the crickets sing. Every once in a while, a frog or two would chime in.

Out of nowhere, Ken offers something about himself, "I love the sound of crickets."

"You do? How come?"

"When I was young, I would open my bedroom window every night and fall asleep to their sounds. I felt completely safe back then. It reminds me of that time in my life."

It was the opening Adelle was looking for. "Is that why you like this place?"

"Never been here before." Those words calm Adelle's mind. He had never brought his wife here. It would be their memory. Walking a little further before Adelle asks another question.

"Do you feel safe now?"

Looking straight ahead, Ken answers, "I don't know what I feel anymore. Safe? Not sure." It was apparent Ken did not want to talk about it further. Adelle takes Ken's arm as they stroll the circular path before returning to their room.

Climbing into bed, they both sink into the soft mattress. Having not spoken much after Adelle's last question, she gently closes her eyes.

"No. I don't," Ken blurts out.

Adelle's eyes pop open. Was Ken already asleep and talking? She turns her head to look and notices in the slight darkness that his eyes are wide open. Turning towards him, she gets up on one elbow to face him but doesn't speak.

"How can anyone feel safe when God can take everything from you in a heartbeat?" His words were dripping in pain. "And there is nothing you can do to stop it." Grief was taking over as Ken continued to express himself. "It's loss. I worry about that. I hid behind my smile every day. I have taught myself to go through the motions and try not to feel."

The honesty crashes in on Adelle. "If you break, I am here."

The offer overwhelms Ken. Immediately he rolls over and faces Adelle. Before even looking into her eyes, he nestles his face in the nape of her neck and sobs quietly. Adelle holds him and gives him the comfort she can.

Whispering to him as if the room is full of others, making her words very intimate. "It hurts. Know I will get you through this. Rest on me."

Her words calmed his heart as his mind began to focus on the harmony of the crickets outside. He was ten all over again.

Morning came quickly. Since they had forgotten to close the curtains the night before, the sunbeams hit like a wake-up call. Sometime during the night, Adelle and Ken had separated and slept on different sides of the bed. Slowly turning to face her, he was surprised that she had been watching him sleep.

"Hey you," Adelle says.

In a groggy voice, Ken replies, "Morning sunshine, Twinkle Toes." With that, she gives him a gentle slap on his shoulder.

"How are you doing this morning?"

"I slept like a baby."

"Sure, you did, Tater." Ken instantly knew this gag would be going on for some time. He knew better than to fight it; after all, he started it this morning.

"Can I ask you something?" Adelle says softly.

Ken could tell it would be a serious question, and he wasn't sure he was up to it after the emotional night. "Can I refuse to answer?'

"Yes, you can."

"Okay."

"Is you helping Mykel, something that helps you deal with the loss of your son?" The question startles Ken a little bit. Considering the question, he begins to think aloud.

"Maybe in some ways. It is like he was brought to me. You know, I didn't seek him out." Ken says as he pushes himself up on a pillow, closer to a sitting position.

"How did you meet then?"

"One of the boys that broke into my house lives across the street. I saw where he lived and parked my car across the street. I was sitting there when Mykel tapped on my car window and asked if I would play catch with him." As he finishes his recollection of events, he turns to face Adelle.

"Do you think he was sent to me?" Ken asks.

"I do," Adelle confirms, but she has another question. "Let me know if this is too much for you, okay? Did you ever think of killing yourself when everything happened?"

Ken rolls over to face her and takes her hand. "No. I did fall into depression; I will admit that. And I still battle it at times. The only reason I never thought about ending my life is because I would end everyone else's. The memories would die with me. Does that make any sense?"

"It does. Can I tell you something?"

"Sure."

"My ex was an abuser. It started with little things —a tug here and a slap there. I thought that I could handle him. Then I got embarrassed that I was staying with him. He took my feeling of safety away from me. I know it is different from yours. But I can understand it from another angle." Taking in a breath, she stops for a few moments. Ken waits patiently as Adelle gets up the courage to continue talking about it. "I am fearful that maybe I can't pick good men. That maybe I should not trust my own choices." Ken takes Adelle into his arms and holds her. Adelle puts her head on Ken's chest. She begins to realize his arms are around her and she loves the way they feel. She closes her eyes to take it all in. Then she continues again. "It took everything I had to walk into your office. If you had looked at me closely, you would have seen me shaking."

"How did I miss that?"

"Ken, you have your own worries."

Stepping back a little, Ken takes both of her hands, he gazes right into her eyes. "Let us do this together. Let us fight the battle together. It won't win."

"Promise." Leaning to seal it with a kiss, Adelle places her lips on his warm and moist mouth. Automatically their bodies press up against each other.

As they are slowly separate, Ken doesn't want to bring up the past fully, but he feels it necessary to let her know why he was so upset about her leaving that night. "Can you understand why walking away from me that night was what I fear most?"

"I can. Again, sorry."

"I'm not trying to keep on the topic. I want you to understand where I went in my brain when that happened." Pausing for a moment before he continues to talk, Ken knows he needs to recognize her words as well. "Thank you for sharing with me about your ex. I get it now."

Changing the topic to a fun topic, Ken gives her a little reminder. "Let's see. We won the game, so..." he trails off.

Jokingly Adelle responds. "Yes, sir. What may I do for you?"

With that, Ken slides back into the bed and throws the sheets off. Adelle reads him like a book.

Snuggling and enjoying each other was what this weekend was all about. After a little roughhousing, they both get up and put on shorts and shirts. It was time for their boat ride around the little lake.

The day was romantic all the way, though. On the drive home after a weekend of pure delight, Adelle had her shoes off and feet up on his dashboard as the wind from the car window tossed her hair. Ken wonders what the weekend would have been like if Adelle had won the bet. With his mind racing, Ken's mind starts spinning. What could he bet her that he could easily lose without giving away that he wants her to win? He would have to come up with something.

"What are you thinking about?" Adelle inquires.

"How nice the weekend was." He replies.

Adelle is not sure he is telling the truth due to the mischievous expression on his face. She decides that there have already been too many questions this weekend and lets it go. The weekend was nice. She was feeling damn good.

CHAPTER TWENTY-FOUR

The weekend of boating, evening walks, and a fantastic couples massage has done well for Ken's attitude. He was feeling light on his feet and loose in his joints. After dropping off Adelle at her house, he was happy to be home for the first time in a long time. As he drove into his driveway, he saw a figure sitting on the low wall surrounding his front porch.

It was a little hard to determine whether he knew the person. The streetlights are not helping his eyesight, and he mentally kicks himself for forgetting to turn on the porch light before he leaves. Before leaving his car, Ken decides he will not take his overnight bag with him if the person has any ill intent.

Getting out of his car, he closes his car door in a way to make more noise than what was necessary. *Bam.*

"Can I help you?" Ken calls out

"Ken. You're home."

Immediately recognizing the voice, Ken realizes it is Mykel. Had he grown over the three days? He looks more like a young man than the young boy that he is.

"What are you doing here? And does your mom know you are here?"

Looking at his feet, Mykel was slightly nervous about answering Ken's questions. "No, she doesn't. I have to talk to you."

Noticing the bike propped up against the opposing wall on the porch, Ken assumes Mykel rode over to his place. Determining Mykel needs help and his luggage can wait, Ken opens his front door and gestures to Mykel to enter.

"First thing is first. We call your mom."

"She doesn't know I am gone. I went out my bedroom window." Ken shoots Mykel a look of disapproval as Mykel keeps talking. "She is always listening to what I am saying. I want to talk with you alone."

"It must be very important for you to go through all this trouble to get here and maybe face the wrath of your mom to do so." It was a roundabout way for Ken to warn Mykel that his mother might know he was gone. "So, what is it?"

"My mom..." Mykel trails off. Ken sits quietly so as not to interrupt. Mykel starts up again. "My mom works hard but doesn't make a lot of money. She makes sure to work hours only when I am in school so she can always be home for me." Listening patiently, Ken was pleased it wasn't a health issue for her.

Looking back at Ken sitting halfway on the couch next to Mykel so he can look him in the face, Mykel locks eyes with Ken before picking up where he left off. "She has just started doing laundry for others." Ken can see the concern in Mykel's eyes. "This is why I think college is out of my reach. She cannot afford to send me."

Understanding more fully why Mykel had little hope of having big dreams became clearer to Ken as Mykel resumed speaking. "What can I do to help?"

"First. Not sneaking out at night and not letting your mom know where you are is a great start." Mykel nods as he glares back at Ken. It was clear that was not the answer Mykel was looking for as he started to roll his eyes but caught himself.

"Will your mom let you have a job? Something like offering to mow some lawns or helping some senior citizens with things like groceries?"

Mykel's expression shifts to deep thought as wonder comes across his face. "She might."

"You need to speak to your mom about your worrying about her. You need to let her know what you are thinking about. As a child, you should not have to worry about such things. I realize you do, though. Can I ask you something?"

"Sure."

"Do you forgo things because you know they cost? Would you go out for a school sport if your mom had the money for the uniforms? Something like that?"

Nodding yes, Mykel begins to feel as if he has become transparent. How did Ken know? Disregarding

Mykel's look, Ken continues. "You know it is very important to talk with your mother. I realize you are trying to help out your mom, but any loving parent does not want to hear you are not participating in things at school because you think your family cannot afford it. I am sure we can work something out, but that will have to involve your mother."

Ken knows Mykel did not want his mom to know he was there, or more importantly, he was talking to Ken about their financial situation. It would be a delicate discussion. "Okay. We will pack up your bike in my car, and let's get you home."

"I can just ride back," Mykel says, almost pleading.

"Sorry. That will not be happening. Come on, let's go."

Ken helps Mykel pop this bike's front wheel so it would fit better in the car. After they load it up, Mykel slides into the passenger seat. As Ken starts to back out of the car, he goes a little slower than normal since Mykel was with him and it was a late Sunday evening.

The notion of drunk drivers at this hour is never far from Ken's mind.

"She is going to kill me. You know that, right?"

"Sneaking out of your room alone at this hour is enough to put you on restriction for some time." Ken offers up. After about two minutes of silence, Ken offers one more bit of advice. "Men own up to their mistakes. And you are her little man."

"Well, I can't wait to be an adult. No one can punish me then." Mykel declares.

With a slight chuckle, Ken disagreed. "That could not be farther from the truth."

"How so?"

"Speeding tickets are a form of punishment. At work, being denied a promotion can be a form of punishment. And if you get married, wives have many ways to tell you when you are in trouble. Believe me." Ken laughs at the last part of his comment. Mykel was a little confused by Ken's laughter but was in no mood to mention it as they pulled up to his house. It would be only a few minutes before he was facing his mother.

Mykel's heart was pounding as he opened the front door. Entering the house, he was surprised to find his mother sitting on the couch waiting for him. A thousand thoughts race through his mind as he tries to figure out when Ken could have called her. There was no way Ken would have been able to call her without him knowing. He determines she already knew he had gone out his window.

Looking at her son with great disappointment, Sonya just sat there waiting for him to talk. She was a little surprised when Ken followed him in the door.

"Mykel, keep going," Ken instructs, standing right behind him to encourage him to do the right thing. "I went over to talk to Mr. Hines. I wanted his help."

Sonya was having none of it. She also did not like Ken's position behind Mykel because she felt it was two against one. "Slipping out your bedroom window was what you thought was the best way to do that?"

"I did not want you to know."

"And why was that?" She asks.

Just standing there, Mykel was not answering. Ken now faces Mykel while maneuvering around him; he still stays out of the line of sight his mother had with her son.

"Mykel, you have to tell her."

Postponing what Mykel knows will be an uncomfortable and possibly humiliating conversation, he struggles to change the topic. "I am sorry I left without telling you. I was wrong."

Ignoring Mykel's words, she asks again, "What did you need to talk to Ken about?"

Looking defeated, Mykel searched for the right words to lessen the impact, but he was taking too long.

"I will not ask you again," his mother states with total authority.

Ken then pushes Mykel to confess. "You are only making it worse. Just start talking like you did with me."

"I... I worry. You work hard. We are destitute. I want to see if I can get a job to help you."

The words struck Sonya's heart. His revelation took her by surprise. Ken stands silently, knowing it is not his place to add to the conversation.

As the words from Mykel reverberated in Sonya's mind, she called him over. "Come here. Sit next to me." She tells her son.

Walking over slowly, he takes his place on the couch and tries not to make direct eye contact with his mother.

"Mykel. I do what I do because I love you. Do you understand that?" Shaking his head yes, Mykel remains wordless. Sonya continues. "I don't want you to worry about making ends meet. That is my job." The compassion in her tone warms Ken's heart. "How long has this bothered you?"

"For a while, I guess."

"How come you didn't tell me? I have always said you can talk to me about anything."

"I know, mom."

"I can't just let this go, Mykel. I was worried about

you."

That was Ken's cue to go. "I think I will go home now and unpack. It was a busy weekend." Neither Mykel nor Sonya acknowledges his words. Ken walks out the front door closing it behind him. He wasn't sure if he would go by Mykel's house the following evening. It might not be appropriate. Thinking it over, he decides he would talk with Adelle tomorrow and get her opinion.

Mykel's words were echoing in Ken's mind. If his son were his age, he would be more than happy to let him do something to earn some cash. What would that something be, he wondered. Mykel had not mentioned any suggestions about what he would want to do to earn money. Mykel was too young for an internship at the office. Newspaper routes are all but gone these days. Odd jobs around a neighborhood would be okay but also came with some risks unless Sonya knew the people he would be working for. Maybe Adelle would have an idea about that too.

Fatigued and depleted, Ken couldn't get in his

bed soon enough. He brought in his luggage and got his coffee ready for the morning. Going upstairs to his room, he only unpacked the items he would need in the morning. Throwing his clothes near his laundry hamper was good enough this night as he slides into bed. Closing his eyes, it was seconds before he was sound asleep. He would sleep through the entire night until his alarm goes off in the morning.

CHAPTER TWENTY-FIVE

Listening to the sound of the phone ringing at the other end of his cell phone brings a little rhythm to Ken's morning. The sound was like a meditation to Ken's mind as it drifts into thoughts of the last several months and how much his life has changed.

"Hello sweetie." Adelle answers.

"Well good morning. How are you?"

"I slept very well last night. You?"

"When I finally got to bed, yes. Listen, I wonder if you can help with a couple of things."

"For the event?" She asks

"That too. Let me tell you about last night. When I got home Mykel was at my house." Ken continues to explain the conversation and what took place. Adelle listens intently to every word. She understands the dilemma Ken was placed in with Mykel coming to his house.

"I am a little at a loss," Ken continues. "Do I go by tonight? Any suggestions on how I can help without causing issues? I don't want to just offer money. I am not trying to be a hero here, but I want to do something."

"That is a lot to unpack." Adelle gathers her thoughts. "If you decide to go by, I don't think playing football would be a good idea. If you go by, you need to address the whole thing. Have you spoken to Mykel about referring to you as his dad yet?"

"No, I haven't. I wanted to speak with Sonya first. I don't know much about his real dad."

"Right. That makes sense. Is there a way you can talk to her first without Mykel around?"

"Not sure. I will have to ask her."

"I would do that first. Then you two decide what to do about it. How do you feel about him calling you dad?"

"I haven't thought about it. On one hand it is nice. On the other, tricky."

"If Sonya is okay with it, then maybe you can find a different term. Pop. Papa. Something affectionate that means the same thing?" Adelle suggests. "Then talk the other stuff through. As for what he can do to earn some money, if Sonya is okay with it, he could tutor younger children with their homework for a small fee."

"Tutoring?"

"Yes. You would be amazed at how many children younger than Mykel need help. It can be done at his house so Sonya can oversee, and often a parent can stay with their child for the hour he is tutoring them if they wish."

"That is a great idea. I love it. You are the best." Ken was beaming. He now has a plan that he feels comfortable with. "Thank you. This will work."

His desk phone begins to ring. "Adelle, can I call you right back?"

"Absolutely. Glad I could help."

It was right there on the tip of his tongue. He almost said it, 'Love you – bye.' "Talk with you later," came out instead.

Hanging up the cell phone, he grabs his desk phone and answers it. "Ken Hines."

"Hey Ken. It's Al."

"Hi Al, what can I do for you today?" Al was one of Ken's favorite clients. Al is the mayor of a neighboring city and had hired Ken to redesign the city offices. They had known each other for years. Al has many connections and has sent many clients to Ken over the years. Being a mayor affords him a lot of business connections in the entire county. He is a great resource to know.

"It is what I can do for you. Instead of the ten trucks you asked for, we got you fifteen."

"That's great news."

"Annd..." Al drags out the word for dramatic effect. "The tree lot is donating 35 trees."

"You have out done yourself again. I appreciate

it." Ken says. The response to Ken's requests to help with his event was overwhelming. Ken has never done anything like this ever. It was getting larger than he could dream.

"Will you be there?" Ken asks

"Family obligations, but I am sure you have it all under control." Al replies.

"Thanks again." Ken immediately calls Adelle back.

"Thanks for letting me take that call. I have some great news." Ken rattles on. He tells her about the trucks and about the trees. Adelle has some of her own good news.

"And I can add to that. The local toy manufacturer has tons they want to donate to us. It includes boy's and girl's toys."

"Not even sure I can put a word to the emotions I am feeling about this whole project. Grateful I guess."

Adelle knows exactly what Ken is talking about, having felt it many times before herself. "I recognize that mixed feeling."

"Letting you know I decided to go over to Mykel's house tonight but to speak with his mother and him later. No tossing a football around right now." Ken wants Adelle to know what he decided.

"Sounds good. I will talk with you later. Someone is donating children's bikes. I will fill you in later. Bye for now."

Ken takes the cue, "Bye. Talk later."

Ken marveled at the fact the drive to Mykel's house was as common as his old drive directly home. So many things had quickly changed in Ken's life, he really didn't contemplate what was taking place. Pulling up to Mykel's house, he found himself greeted by the little man. Soon his mother was standing at the door as Ken approached.

"Any chance I can speak with you alone?" Ken asks Sonya.

"Certainly. Little man, the adults have to talk." Mykel knew what that sentence means and goes out back to occupy himself with a frisbee. Ken walks in and sits at the kitchen table with Sonya.

"I have wanted to talk with you alone for a while. This is all strange to me and I feel a little uncomfortable about a couple of things." Sonya nods knowingly in agreement.

Continuing he said, "My first concern is the fact that Mykel had referred to me a couple of times as his dad. I want to talk to him about it, but I would like your feelings about it first."

"I have heard that. His dad died of an illness when Mykel was barely one year old. He has never really known him, or really had any male figures in his life. His dad has brothers, but they have never come around or stepped up to help us. I have all sisters. One is married, but they have their own children that keep them very busy." Sonya watches Ken's reaction as she tells him her thoughts. "It is a little strange to hear him call you that, but I am more concerned if the time comes that you have to walk away that he will not be losing another so-called dad."

That thought had never crossed Ken's mind. He

is worrying more about Sonya and not knowing where Mykel's real dad lives could be an issue if he returns. Now knowing he had passed away, that fear was gone.

"I am so sorry to hear that. Know that I understand your concern. Also know I don't have any intentions of leaving or even moving away. I don't take my loyalty lightly." Ken commits.

Thinking about Sonya's words, he resumes the discussion. "Well maybe we can compromise by giving me a nickname of some sorts that only you and Mykel use?"

"That sounds terrific. I like that idea." Sonya agrees.

"Great. Then there is the coming to my house late at night. I was not happy about that. But Mykel talking about worrying about you is very sweet. However, sneaking out of a house is something I would not tolerate, and I am sure you were not very happy."

"He got punished. He has more chores right now and will have to forego playing outside for a while. Know though, that we did have a good talk about the issue. I had no idea he was that worried about my working so hard. I am not sure I calmed his fears so maybe you can help."

"Know he never asked me for money. He asked what he could do to earn money. I do respect that."

"That is good to hear. I raised him right that way." Sonya says.

Beaming with a little pride, Ken explains, "Adelle has a great idea to make a little cash." Sonya's eyes widen in interest. "She suggests that he can tutor younger children. One, he can do it out of your home and two, a parent can either stay with their children or just wait in the car outside."

"That is a great idea. I like it." Sonya sports a giant smile. "That will certainly help him feel like he is doing something, and he is so good with younger kids in the neighborhood. It would be perfect."

"Shall we tell him together?" Ken asks.

"No. Go right ahead and let him know he has my blessing."

After hugging each other, Ken walks out to the backyard and calls Mykel over to talk. Sitting in a couple of chairs, Mykel actually starts.

"I'm still in trouble, right?" Mykel questions.

"A little, yes. I am sure your mother gave you a stern talking to, but I want you to know it wasn't coming to talk to me that was the issue. It was the sneaking out of the house and the late hour." Ken looks directly into Mykel's eyes making his point stronger.

"I know. I won't do that again. I promised mom."

"Good. Also, I would prefer we come up with a nickname for me instead of directly calling me your dad. Not that I would not love to be your dad, but I think people get confused easily when we do that."

"Like what?" Mykel asks.

"Hmm. Paw? Step dude?" Ken cringes at the suggestions.

"Awful. How about big guy? If I am little man, you can be the big guy."

"Big guy. Sounds okay to me." Ken laughs. Ken

goes on to explain about the suggestion Adelle had made.

"How do you feel about tutoring children younger with their homework?" Ken asks.

"I kind of do that now and then for others."

"Why not officially? You can charge a small fee and help your mother out." Ken offers.

"I can do that. My mom is okay with it?"

"She sure is."

"Let's make up a little flyer and you can hand it out to neighbors and maybe post it at your school. Sound good?" Mykel jumps up and heads to the back door.

"What are you waiting for?" Mykel asks.

Laughing as he answers, "Nothing," Ken follows Mykel back into the house.

CHAPTER TWENTY-SIX

Half the day flew by before Ken even realized it. The new position of Vice-President came with a lot of other tasks Ken was not really ready for or preferred. He was happiest being able to work with younger architects in the firm and made sure to schedule time with anyone who desires his help.

Just as Ken clears his throat Carol shows up at his door.

"Come on in." Ken says, welcoming her. "How is your day going?" Ken always likes to ask how the people who work for him are doing personally. Many employees respect Ken for this mindset.

"I'm doing well. Thanks for asking. I need your advice." Carol says

"Sure. Tell what you are working on while you

show me the current plans."

"It is a new media center. They want to ensure areas and designs for people to use mini studios for podcasting and other social media. On this side we have some areas that are individual with different colored walls and some unique designs. Over here, a little down the hall, there is a larger studio with options of green or blue screen walls. To the side area are the buildings with offices for the people that work there with their break area."

"Sounds good so far. What are you concerned about?" Ken asks.

"Two things. I feel like something is missing, and windows can be a problem for people filming, but we don't want everything solid."

"How about adding an open collaboration area where little groups of people can be in a more open area with some walls that are white boards? Lots of color in the table and chairs."

"Oh, I love that. Yes. We could put that in this area." Carol confirms as she marks up the plans.

"Will there be snacks, coffee bar, juice bar, area for people to stay and hang around for a while?"

"I can expand the area over here for that. There are windows in this area."

"Extend it to outdoors and use some gardening to make the boarders. Also, for the windows, how about skylights that can remotely close when needed? They allow light and darkness."

Carol was grinning. All these ideas made her very excited to go back to her desk and add these ideas into her design. Just as she is about to thank Ken for his suggestions, his assistant walks in.

"Sorry to interrupt. A Ms. Sonya needs you to call her. Right away."

"Thank you. Carol do you need anything else?"

"No. I appreciate your time. May I bring it back once I get the design tighter?"

"Absolutely. I would love to see what you do with it."

Not rushing her but escorting her out the door,

he goes back to his desk and calls Mykel's mom from his cell phone. After the first ring, Sonya is already on the phone. "Hello."

"Hi. I was told you needed me to call you. Everything okay?" Ken asks.

"Can you come by please? I need you to speak with Mykel. I will tell you when you get here."

"Is he okay?" Ken becomes concerned. Sneaking a peak at his calendar, he notices he is clear for the rest of the day. "I can come now."

"See you soon."

Excusing himself from his office and letting his assistant know he would be gone for the rest of the day but is available by phone if needed, Ken hustles out to his car. He heads directly over to the Alder's.

Mykel is not outside playing in the yard as Ken would have expected. Maybe because it is a little earlier in the weekday than Ken usually comes over. Ken is not sure that is the real reason, but until he hears about what is happening, he will wait to find out.

Knocking on the front door, Sonya answers.

"Come in. Come in."

Entering the house, he is directed to the couch. He still does not see Mykel, but he does notice that Mykel's bedroom door is closed. Wondering what Mykel has done now, he turns his attention back to Sonya.

"What happen today?" Ken inquires.

"Sex education class was today." Sonya says with a straight face. Ken could not stop his reaction fast enough, as his eyes bulges out a little and his face starts to turn a little red. He was just hit with an eighteen-wheeler truck. This was something he had totally forgotten about having lost his son before he ever came of age for this discussion. Now Ken was wishing Sonya had warned him before he got there. He needs time to think.

"Not sure what you need from me." Ken asks sheepishly.

"He has questions. Guess he has had some questions for a while now. But he doesn't want to talk to me. He said he would talk to you." Sonya advises Ken, who is a little panicky at this point. Still a little speechless, Sonya fills the room with more conversation. "I don't want him learning from the internet. There is too much there, and it is too confusing."

That had not even occurred to Ken yet. Rubbing the sweat from both palms of his hands on his pants, Ken agrees to go speak with Mykel.

"He wants to talk tonight?" Ken askes

"Yes. He is in his room."

Standing up slowly. Ken looks back at Sonya. As if reading his mind, she lets him know she is confident that he can handle it. "Speak from your heart and experiences. Just be honest. That is all I care about."

Walking up to Mykel's door, Ken knocks on it. "Mykel, it is the big guy."

Ken heard a muffled, "Come in." Entering the room, Ken made sure to close the door behind him. Even though he had been in Mykel's room before, he didn't really look it over last time. Looking around the room, Ken saw it was sparingly furnished. He has a small single bed with some older bedspreads, a basic desk, chair, and a modest bookcase. He did have a computer on his desk, which when Ken spotted it brought a little relief but also some fear. Mykel was sitting in his chair by his desk. Ken walks over to the bed to sit on the edge.

"I know the basics. So don't go there." Mykel said.

"Sure. Okay. Is there something you want to discuss?" Ken asks.

"Yes." Mykel seems to be examining his shoes in order to avoid direct eye contact with Ken. "Can girls get pregnant even when they don't get excited?"

Ken was a little taken aback that Mykel had that as a first question. "Absolutely they can. Being excited does not release the egg. Women have cycles when the eggs are released. Therefore, yes they can get pregnant by the act of intercourse." Ken took in a breath. He knew he dodged a bullet but wasn't sure the line of questioning was over.

"Does that make sense Mykel?"

"They taught us about that." Mykel pauses for a moment. Tilting his head up he asks another question as he points to his crotch, "Has mine stopped growing? Will it get any bigger?"

Ken knew that question well. Probably every young man has wondered, but most probably would never ask. "You are still a growing young man. Many parts of you will continue to grow until your 18, 19, 20-ish." Letting it sink in for a moment before he continues with the fear most young men have and knowing Mykel probably wouldn't ask anyways.

"You know your being a man is not determined by size, right?"

Mykel rolls his eyes. "In the locker room it is." Mykel gives Ken a questioning look.

Ken finishes. "Yes, even that." It was hard for Ken to hide the smile he was feeling inside. Ken was still a bit nervous and wipes his hands on his pants again. He could see the Mykel was getting up the courage to ask another question.

"Go ahead. You know I was your age once. I had a lot of questions for my dad."

"You did?"

"Sure, I did. I was just like you. You learn as you grow up. What else did you want to ask me?"

"Sometimes it is difficult to control. How do you handle that?" Mykel asks.

"You are right. That will get better with time. But if you find yourself with an erection at an awkward time, sit down if you can. Or excuse yourself to the restroom. Know that it happens to all of us at one time or another."

"Does it happen to women too?" Mykel wonders

"Sure. But unlike us, we cannot tell. It is not a visible reaction." Thinking about what he would tell his own son if he were here, Ken decides to continue to speak. "Don't let anyone pressure you into having sex if you are not ready. And I am sure you understand how important it is to protect yourself and your partner."

Shaking his head in agreement, Mykel remains quiet. Ken could see he was thinking everything through. Waiting a few minutes, Ken finally asks, "Do you have any more questions for now?"

"How do you know when it is the right time? And

how do you know the girl wants it too?"

"It will be easier when you are older. Speaking from experience, I can tell you that it is worth the wait. I can also tell you that you will know when someone actually loves you by their actions. There is sex, the act of doing it. And there is love, the intimate act of sharing your bodies and minds. Most make the mistake of doing the first one for their first experience and it normally turns out being a bad one."

Ken can tell Mykel had truly been listening to every word. Ken knows it does not make full sense to him at his young age, but he will remember the words. "Any other questions?"

"No."

"Be careful of what is on the internet. Your mom and I would prefer you speak with us about any issue. Okay?"

"Teachers said that too." Mykel states.

Leaving the bedroom, Ken walks out in silence. Feeling that there will more of these talks to come. He also did not want to break Mykel's confidence, so he only spoke in generalities when describing what they discussed.

"He is a normal inquisitive boy. Nothing unusual." Ken explains.

That was all Sonya needed to hear. She was happy that Ken came over and spent time with her son. She offers him dinner, but he decides to go home. Ken could not put his finger on his emotions as they were a cross between being sad this discussion was not with his own son, and elated that Mykel felt he was the one to turn to.

CHAPTER TWENTY-SEVEN

With the holiday season here, the office was decorative, and food was available on almost every desk in the office. The break area of the building was a dieter's worse nightmare. Ken always had the ability to pass it all by. As someone who watches what he eats, he doesn't eat much to begin with at all. Everyone is feeling light and enjoying the festivities.

Ken's assistant comes into his office and walks over to the globe. Giving it a huge spin, she stood there watching it spin. Ken was sitting at his desk answering emails, and stops to watch the globe swirl at a high speed. As it starts to reduce in speed, Ken speaks out.

"Did you come in here just for that?"

"Actually no. The spinning was to give me the courage to ask you a personal question."

"Oh really? That does take courage."

The assistant walks over to the chair in front of his desk and takes a seat on the end of the chair cushion, leaning in a little towards him.

"What is going on in your life? Is there someone?" she questions.

"Before I answer you, tell me the rumors."

"Rumors?" She acts innocently.

"Stop stalling. No rumors, no answers."

Smiling, his assistant understood how right he is and begins to talk. "You have a lady friend. The woman from the charity. Is that true?"

"Interesting. What if I tell you there is more than one?" Ken implies.

"You are dating more than one woman?" Surprising the assistant.

"Go off the deep end. Didn't say I was dating anyone. But I am dating one of them."

"Stop with the games. Come on tell me." The

assistant begs.

"I'm a very private person. Everyone knows that."

"Is she pregnant?"

"What? No!" Ken knows rumors spin uncontrollable and maybe answering her question would extinguish the stories. "Yes, I am dating Adelle. I also have started mentoring a young man which has brought a lot of joy to my life."

"Are you going to marry her? Have you told her you love her?"

"Now you are getting too personal. That is all you and the staff need to know." Ken advises.

"Got it. Let's just say whatever is happening in your life, we all love it. You have changed. We missed the old Ken. Your silly jokes, smiles, and just being sociable."

"Can I bring her to the office holiday party, or all you all going to jump her?" Ken askes.

"I will tell them to all be on their best behavior,"

the assistant states as she gets out of the chair and heads towards his door.

"Tell them all to act better than that or I am not bringing her."

"Will do boss."

Several days later the office holiday party was in full swing. Ken brought the beautiful Adelle. She was dressed in a gorgeous evening dress in a gorgeous blue and ivory satin. A slit that goes right above her knee is adorned with an embroidered multi-green shaded dragonfly that gives the appearance of holding the dress together. Her see-through thin wrap has small matching dragonflies embroidered all throughout the shawl. Her hair was pulled back with some matching Australian crystal hair clips. She was elegant.

Everyone knew that she and Ken make for a perfect looking couple. He tends to her like she is a princess. Several women are a little envious but certainly can understand her attraction to him. Ken made sure to make the rounds, introducing her to the other employees who had not officially met her before. Upper management all knew who she was. She worked the crowd accordingly as Ken had prepared her beforehand. She understands how the gossip machine works and stayed about the fray.

In all honesty, Ken could have stayed home before, but being a top executive now, that was no longer an option. Leaving early was though. As soon as Ken felt it was safe to go, he and Adelle snuck out. Slipping into his car, he grabs his tie and loosen it.

"Can I tell you again that you look amazing?" Ken offers up.

"Thank you. I did my best. And you are looking dapper. I love being on your arm."

"You love that?"

Adelle looks at him as he seems focused on his driving. But he was really focused on her. "How slowly I can take that dress off. You are my present under the tree, right?" He asks.

Adelle starts to giggle a little. "Bad boys get coal Ken." The conversation goes quiet. Ken couldn't think of a fast enough comeback that was up to his standard.

It didn't matter anyways. He knows it didn't matter if he was going to be good or going to be bad. They were going to have fun.

Once back to her place, Adelle kicks off her shoes. Taking his left hand, as she walks a bit backwards, she leads him to her bedroom. Getting out of these tight and confining clothes would bring a few freedoms.

The evening was everything Ken and Adelle, both dreamed it would be. The evening was hot for a winter's night. Ken was on the verge again of saying the commitment word, but he still holds back. Laying there almost exhausted, while his mind would not turn off. He wonders why he doesn't just say it. It bothers him. Searching his gut, he may be afraid to cross that threshold, opening himself up to the possibility of losing someone again. He explores his options until his eyes close for the night. Adelle was asleep an hour earlier.

The morning light brought the new day and Christmas Eve. Ken and Adelle rose early as they have a lot of items to pull together. Ken heads over to a large warehouse as Adelle stays home to make some last-minute calls and reminders.

Directing everyone seems natural to Ken. "Steve, line these up over there so we can just place them on the trucks."

Someone yells out, "The trucks are here."

The urgency of every task increases. Rolling up his sleeves, Ken helps to load the trucks. Everything had been nicely prepared earlier by Adelle's volunteers and her team.

Soon Adelle arrives and pitches in. Going through her list, she checks off all the boxes, making sure everything that was promised has arrived and been divvied up evenly into each of the fifteen trucks.

Before heading out, everyone stops and gathers around in a large circle. Ken takes center stage. "First I want to thank each and every one of you for making this happen. I cannot begin to express my gratitude for the donations and your time. What we are doing here today is bringing joy to others. I pray you find as much joy, if not more, than I do, for this day."

"Hoorah!" was heard from one person. Then a second one was heard with several more joining in. "Hoorah." Then everyone joins in on the third one. "Hoorah."

"Let's do this." Ken shouts.

With that the workers and volunteers jump into the back of the trucks as the drivers close the back and jump in starting their trucks. Like a giant convoy, the trucks in single file head down the four-lane road. Five minutes later, they are at their destination. The first truck pulls to the end of the street, while each truck lines up directly behind the one in front of it.

Ken and Adelle pull up next door to Mykel's house and remain in their car. Sitting back, they watch the magic unfold.

The driver's pop out of their cabs and all open the back of their trucks. Drivers head back to their cabs, turning on their radios and turning up the sound. The music penetrated the entire neighborhood, calling out every resident that was home. They begin to emerge from the front of their homes and all watch from their front yards in an attempt to figure out what was going on.

People dressed as elves jump out of the back of every semi-trailer bed. A few people inside the truck move trees to the lift as the elves outside lower it. Like clockwork, each truck begins to empty as the elves bring the goodies over to each house. They fill their yards with trees, presents, and groceries for each family at each house on the street.

Sonya had heard the noise too and was standing outside watching the spectacle as a few elves brought over two fully decorated trees, several presents to put under the tree, and food for a huge holiday feast. Mykel had been in his room until he hears all the ruckus. Running outside to see what was happening, he takes in the pageantry happening on his entire street.

Children all along the street start yelling for joy. They are hopping and skipping around. A couple grab bikes with the ribbons still on them and start to ride them up and down the street. Younger kids are riding their trikes on the sidewalks.

Parents are creating little groups and are asking how this is all happening. There were no signs of who was giving them all fantastic gifts and holiday treats. They were bewildered but were loving every second.

Then there was a tapping on Ken's passenger window. This time it was Sonya and Mykel waiting there for them to get out of the car.

"Shall we?" Adelle asks.

"Why not?" Ken grabs three gifts from the back seat. Then he and Adelle step out of the car. Ken joins Sonya, Mykel, and Adelle on the sidewalk in front of the neighbor's house.

"Here you go Mykel." Ken hands him the gifts. Looking at his mom, she signals that it is okay to open it now. He digs in. His eyes open wide when he realizes it is the latest football shoes with cleats. Mykel is so excited. He rushes in to hug Ken.

"It is from Adelle too." Ken says. Mykel turns to hug Adelle as well. Then he dives into the second present. Not believing his eyes, he was on the verge of crying. A brand-new computer. Even his mother was surprised.

"That's too much." Sonya says. Ken shakes his head no. "For his studies. By the way Mykel, I had them load the newest design software."

"Really?" Mykel says more from excitement than a real question.

Adelle hands Sonya a gift as well.

"Thank you. You guys didn't have to." Sonya says. She begins opening the gift. Adelle helps by grabbing the wrapping paper so Sonya can open the box. Her eyes expand as she realizes what she is looking at. Pulling it from the box, she shakes it free. It is a full-length red felt coat in the classic style. It is stunning. She immediately throws it on and spins like a model.

"This is too much."

Adelle is smiling. "It fits you perfectly."

Sonya comes over and gives Adelle a huge embrace and then Ken. She was feeling like the queen of the neighborhood. She couldn't wait to show it off to everyone. Turning her attention to all the activities on the street. "This is you, isn't it?" Sonya asks.

Putting his hand to his chest, he asks, "Me?"

"This is amazing. I have never witnessed such joy." Sonya explains.

"Please don't tell anyone who you think it is. It took a lot of people to pull this off. Adelle here is a great organizer. I cannot rightfully say it was me."

"It was your idea." Adelle adds.

"Well, nothing would have happened without you, my love." Ken replies. He immediately realizes the words he chose. It was out there now. That word he that scared him a little. He notices he didn't mind it at all. It was easier than he thought it would be and his concern disappeared.

Facing Ken, Sonya puts both hands on each of his shoulders and looks him dead in the eyes. "Never in my dreams did I imagine this. No one here will ever forget it." Sonya finishes with a huge embrace.

Becoming engulfed in sensations that are just too much for Ken to handle, he turns away from everyone in the yard. He needs a moment, to gather his heart and head, and push his emotions down.

Turning back around too soon, his feelings got the best of him. All this happiness was taking its toll on Ken. He wishes to finish the day off in style.

"Adelle." Ken calls out. She turns to look at him. With all the happy turmoil going on in the background, Ken takes her left hand. Going down on one knee, Ken looks up at her. Adelle is astonished.

"When I think of you, I know you hold my heart in a protective space. You are intelligent, loving and one of the most compassionate people I know. You have been open with me and I hope I have been open with you. You deserve all your dreams, someone who will support you without limits, encourage you to continue to grow, and love you endlessly. Will you let me be the one?" Ken pulls out a ring from his pocket.

Adelle was shaking her head yes. "Yes. Yes. Yes." She leans in to hug him as he lifts her from the ground.

Sonya and Mykel were applauding. Quickly they were all hugging each other. Adelle could not have found a more romantic time and place. It meant everything to her. As Ken and Adelle stand arm in arm, they turn to watch the festivities along the entire street. It is a remarkable sight as the entire neighborhood was cheerful and happy. The children were playing as the trucks, now empty, drive away. Children fill the street with all their new toys. It was a holiday like none other.

How it happened remains a mystery. Sonya and Mykel never let on who the Santa Claus could be. They act as mystified as everyone else. Some think it was that guy with the flag football game, but Sonya says she doesn't think so. When Mykel ask her how she can lie, she reminds him Ken said it wasn't him really.

EPILOGUE

Over the next few years, Ken and Mykel grew even closer. Ken, along with Mykel's mother, guide Mykel through the many obstacles of growing up, asking out his first girl on a date, and getting his first car. Ken was very influential in helping Mykel get a used car.

As Mykel finishes his public schooling, with Ken's continued mentoring, his grades were better than anyone may have expected. Mykel was very proud of his accomplishments. His great grades and extra-curricular activities, gives him the opportunity to attend the college of his choice.

Following his dream of becoming an architect, Mykel decides follow in Ken's footsteps by attending Ken's alma mater on a partial scholarship along with the funds Ken and Mel had set aside for their own child.

A year after proposing to Adelle, their wedding

ceremony was elegant but simple. Spending their honeymoon in the fanciest hotel in the French quarter of New Orleans. Walking the streets and visiting all the shops was a relaxing exploration of Cajun food and pirate's treasure. The trip gave them a lot of time talking and getting to know each other even better.

Following their marriage, Adelle and Ken gave birth to a baby girl they name Melissa Sue, in honor of Ken's late wife. It was a complete pleasure for the couple to start a new college fund for their baby girl.

When Melissa is three months old, Ken and Adelle bring her to the cemetery to share their new her with Melissa and Clint. It means everything to Ken to share his wife's namesake to let Melissa and Clint know they will never be forgotten.

Adelle continues to grow her charity work. 'Celebrate A Street' Foundation becomes a nationwide program with branches in all major cities. Ken is at her side every step of the way.

When Mykel finally graduates from college, he takes a job as a junior Architect working for Morgan at the same firm as Ken.

Ken realizes that somewhere along his personal journey he had become a lot like his own mentor Mr. Woodruff though he had never seen himself in that way. How he was the one in the big office mentoring a younger Architect or two.

Taking it all in, Ken re-examines his current state of affairs as he finds himself sitting at Mr. Woodruff's desk, staring out the window. He is married, with a family. *How did this all happen?* He wonders as the expression of joy breaks out on his face. He never saw it coming.

As Ken continues to reflect on his life, his protégé Mykel enters his office to discuss a current project. Immediately Ken gets a mischievous smirk as he turns to face Mykel.

"So, tell me Mykel, have you ever wanted to spin that globe?"

ABOUT THE AUTHOR

A storyteller by her very nature, Kay A. Oliver has been creative her whole life. An avid reader and writer, she has begun focusing on her own stories to share in hopes of bringing joy to those that read her work. Her easy-to-read style makes her books page-turners that are full of twists you never see coming.

Kay A. Oliver was a prolific writer in the entertainment industry, and she has been writing since her youth, winning many different awards in the course of her career. Now she is following her passion for authoring fictional books. Her fictional series "Voice of A Mummy" won her first place in the Spring 2022 Bookfest Writing Awards.

This book, being her latest page-turner, leaves nothing to doubt. Her writing style and Hollywood experience never deliver a dull moment. Her ability and her imagination is quickly making her a legendary storyteller of our time.

Kay A. Oliver graduated from California State University, Fullerton with a Communication: Radio, TV, Film degree, before working in Hollywood for a few decades. During that time, she obtained her master's degree in Business, Finance. She is still a current member of the TV Academy.

Made in the USA
Monee, IL
01 November 2023

45621750R00184